"This
packed

"Prio
t

"Na

"The a
escape
good

JU

"So exciting I coul
TOW

D1494104

JUNIOR

Please return/renew this item by the last date shown

worcestershire
countycouncil
Libraries & Learning

7000374

Artemisian Throne a 'Political Time Bomb'

DR JEREMY BRYAN, lecturer in Government at the Royal Artemisia University, has raised questions about who will succeed to the throne, following rumours that Papa King (*pictured above, before his stroke*) is in failing health.

Dr Bryan says that people need to remember that the next king or queen of Artemisia will be the person named by Papa King in his will, not necessarily Papa King's daughter, Madame.

'His daughter Karen, whom we know as Madame, has lived outside of Artemisia for many years, and only returned after her father became ill. There was clearly some sort of rift there, so I don't think we can assume Papa King has left the throne to her,' Dr Bryan said. 'Frankly, in recent years, he has been much closer to Rosamund and Emily Miniver.'

Dr Bryan refused to say who might have been named in the will as Papa King's successor, but said that it was important that the Parliament of Artemisia look into what he termed 'a political time bomb'.

SUPPORT FOR THE MINIVERS BOUNCES BACK

Support for missing pop princesses Emily and Rosamund Miniver appears to have bounced back, following a mysterious broadcast by a person claiming to be Rosamund Miniver.

Popular TV interviewer Serena Simpson recently claimed that the Minivers were selfish and extravagant. Her accusations were followed by a top-rating documentary, *Inside Miniver House*, detailing the miniature sisters' outrageously luxurious lifestyle. The reports caused widespread anger and riots in some parts of Artemisia. But though the Minivers' reputation suffered badly, a recent opinion poll shows that support for the Minivers has jumped from a low 23 percent to 41 percent of the population.

The official Minivers Fan Club has been quiet since the allegations. However, long-time fan and founder of the Friends of Rosamund Club, Jared Kingsley, says that the stories are nothing but lies and exaggerations.

'The Minivers' real fans will always stick by them,' said Mr Kingsley. 'I am more worried about what is happening to Rosamund and Emily. I pray every night that they will be found safe and well.'

PAPA KING'S CONDITION UNCHANGED

RECENT RUMOURS about the worsening health of Artemisia's ruler, Papa King, are untrue, according to a palace spokeswoman.

'Papa King's condition is basically unchanged,' said palace spokeswoman, Miss Adelaide Clark. 'He is receiving around-the-clock medical care from his nursing staff, and is comfortable. There is no suggestion that he needs to be transferred to a hospital.'

Papa King suffered a severe stroke a year ago. Since then, he has remained a reclusive invalid in the Artemisia Palace, and has not been seen in public. His daughter, Madame, aged 31, has taken over most of the day-to-day government on his behalf.

RADIO ARTEMISIA BACK ON AIR

TOP LOCAL STATION, Radio Artemisia, is back on air after a group of teenage girls attempted to hijack the station on the weekend.

The four girls, who were all residents at the Queen Rosamund Home for Delinquent Girls, broke out of the home on Saturday night. It is believed that all four were devoted fans of the Minivers.

'The girls told me they wanted to get the Minivers back on the air,' said technician, Simon Peeble, who was working late when the girls broke into the station. 'They were like animals. They tied me to a chair and threatened to burst my eardrums with loud Minivers music unless I helped them.'

The intruders succeeded in broadcasting several Minivers songs, and a speech by a person claiming to be Rosamund Miniver. However, a spokeswoman from Operation Miniver, Ms Primrose McLennan, has said the speech was probably made by an imposter.

'I know Rosamund Miniver's voice very well, and it wasn't her,' she said. 'I think we are dealing with deluded fans, here. The real Rosamund has been missing for weeks. By now she is probably dead.'

The four girls were taken into custody by police, and have since been returned to the Queen Rosamund Home.

WOMAN MISSING AFTER SUSPICIOUS FIRE

Police are calling for the owner of a house destroyed by fire in Artemisia West to come forward after reports that the blaze was caused by arson.

The wooden cottage in Daventry Street was nearly a hundred years old. It was unoccupied at the time of the fire, but is believed to have belonged to Livia Wallace, 25, an employee at the City Archives.

Ms Wallace's car was later discovered, abandoned and damaged, near the Royal Artemisia Golf Course. Police have confirmed that she did not turn up for work on Monday morning. They are concerned for her safety, and ask anyone who knows of her whereabouts to contact them urgently.

SECURITY UPGRADED AFTER GRAFFITI ATTACKS

Security at a number of Artemisia railway stations has been increased, following a spate of graffiti attacks late last week.

Artemisia Rail confirmed that several thousand dollars worth of damage was done to rolling stock, and that other railway property has been defaced with slogans. The attacks have been blamed on a group calling itself the 'Minivers Underground'.

'They appear to be extreme fans, who were unhappy to hear recent negative news reports about their idols,' said rail security specialist, Neil Carmichael.

Mr Carmichael said that anyone caught damaging railway property would be prosecuted to the full extent of the law.

KITTY
The most economical cat food on the market.

Especially formulated. As used at the palace by Madame.

Natalie Jane Prior was born in Brisbane, Australia, in November, 1963. Her father is English, and her mother Australian. As a child, she spent most of her time with her nose in a book, or writing doll-sized stories for her friends during maths lessons. She made up her mind to be a children's author when she was about ten, and although she worked for a while as a librarian for a gold-mining company, she has never seriously wanted to do anything else.

Natalie published her first book, *The Amazing Adventures of Amabel,* in 1990. Since then she has written picture books, prize-winning novels and even a best-selling book about mummies! Some of her other books include *The Paw* (illustrated by Terry Denton), a picture book about a cat burglar, and the *Lily Quench* series, which has been published in many countries around the world. Natalie started working on the *Minivers* because she wanted to write a book about what it's like to be on the run when you're only two feet tall and everyone knows what you look like.

Natalie lives in Brisbane with her husband and daughter and two miniature dachshunds called Rupert and Jasmine, in a house with a dragon on the roof.

Also by **Natalie Jane Prior**

the MINIVERS
ON THE RUN

the MINIVERS
IN DANGER

the MINIVERS

AND THE SECRET ROOM

Natalie Jane Prior

MARION LLOYD BOOKS

First published in the UK in 2010 by Marion Lloyd Books
An imprint of Scholastic Children's Books
Euston House, 24 Eversholt Street
London, NW1 1DB, UK
A division of Scholastic Ltd.
Registered office: Westfield Road, Southam, Warwickshire, CV47 0RA
SCHOLASTIC and associated logos are trademarks and/
or registered trademarks of Scholastic Inc.

Copyright © Natalie Jane Prior, 2010
First published in Australia by Pearson Australia Group Pty Ltd, 2010
The right of Natalie Jane Prior to be identified as the author
of this work has been asserted by her.

ISBN 9781407110462

A CIP catalogue record for this book
is available from the British Library

All rights reserved
This book is sold subject to the condition that it shall not,
by way of trade or otherwise, be lent, hired out or otherwise circulated in any form
of binding or cover other than that in which it is published. No part of this
publication may be reproduced, stored in a retrieval system, or transmitted in any
form or by any means (electronic, mechanical, photocopying, recording or
otherwise) without the prior written permission of Scholastic Limited.

Printed by CPI Bookmarque Ltd, Croydon, Surrey
Papers used by Scholastic Children's Books are made
from wood grown in sustainable forests.

1 3 5 7 9 10 8 6 4 2

This is a work of fiction. Names, characters, places, incidents and dialogues
are products of the author's imagination or are used fictitiously. Any resemblance
to actual people, living or dead, events or locales is entirely coincidental.

www.scholastic.co.uk/zone

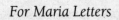
For Maria Letters

1
THE ESCAPE

Emily Miniver saw the spotlight moving towards her. Warm light streamed through the darkness as if it were alive. The light hit Emily's body and she swung automatically to face it. Emily had grown up in the spotlight, and it had always been her friend.

In that moment she was on stage again, holding her sister Rosamund's hand, while the audience shouted "Rosamund!" and "Emily!" and "Minivers for ever!" Emily saw the mass of fans filling the vast bowl of the cricket ground, felt the ecstatic rush of their applause and the vibration of their twenty thousand eager, drumming feet. The words of her next song rose to her lips, and her body tensed as if to launch into a dance. Then the moving spotlight swung up and hit her full in the face. A single shout went up from the palace grounds below and all at once she was no longer Emily Miniver, miniature superstar, but a desperate fugitive, trying to escape.

Emily turned and fled the spotlight. She had hoped to get off the roof of the Artemisia Palace before her captors noticed she was gone, but it seemed she had not been as clever as she thought. For twenty-four hours, Emily had been held prisoner by Madame, the daughter of Artemisia's ruler, Papa King. Madame was trying to steal her father's throne, and it was because Emily and Rosamund were the old king's foster daughters that they had been forced to go on the run.

The spotlight dipped and wavered after her tiny figure. Emily's first instinct was to run back to the chimney through which she had made her escape, but the moment she reached it, she realized it was a hopeless hiding place. Someone would find a ladder, and she could not go back inside the building. Emily zigzagged away again, this time up the sloping roof. Her trainers squeaked and slipped on the metal, her breath panted in and out, and her leg muscles screamed with the steepness of the climb. At the top of the roof, she scrambled over the ridge-capping on to the other side. The spotlight was still raking back and forth above the roof line. Keeping low and out of sight, Emily ran to the end of the metal roof and jumped like a cat on to a tiled one.

She had to get off the rooftops, but she did not know where to go. There was no way down, and she was not even certain where she was. A voice cried out, and Emily heard the sound of pounding feet. The roofs were like a mountain range in front of her, all steep slopes, running down to dangerous chasms between the cluster of buildings. Emily laboured uphill, away from the voice, but this was the oldest part of the palace and the tiles clunked and shifted dangerously under her feet. She reached another roof-ridge, but as she vaulted over it, a tile broke and pitched her off balance. Emily cried out. Her arms flung up in a desperate attempt to stop herself falling, and then she was tumbling rapidly over and over, down the roof to the bottom. One hand grabbed the gutter as she bounced over the edge, and a second later she landed with a jarring thump among some hydrangeas.

"Ouch!" For a moment Emily sat under the giant leaves, catching her breath. Her hands and knees were grazed and oozing blood, but the fall had merely knocked the breath out of her. Minivers were tiny, only two feet tall, but though they were smaller than everyone else, their little bodies were toughly built. The hydrangeas had taken a worse punishing than Emily had, and luckily she had landed in soft, newly dug soil. Emily stood up. She would have preferred to sit and catch her breath, but it was only a matter of time before the people with the spotlight arrived on this side of the

3

building. There was a low sash window above her head, and it was open just enough for her to squeeze through. Emily clawed her way up on to the sill and dropped down into a dimly lit room inside the royal palace.

It was cold. A strange chemical smell filled Emily's nostrils, like a mixture of medicine and disinfectant, and she saw she was standing in a private hospital room with a single bed and one patient. The shadowy figure of a man with a high forehead and a beak of a nose was lying against the crisp white pillows, surrounded by monitors and softly humming equipment. His mouth was slightly open, and there was a steady hiss from an oxygen bottle that stood on a trolley beside the bed.

For a moment, Emily hesitated. She had not been here before, but she knew where she was. The man in the bed was Papa King, the ruler of all Artemisia, and Rosamund and Emily Miniver's foster father. Nearly a year ago, a stroke had left him unable to talk or even move. Emily had not seen him since his return from hospital: after Rosamund's one visit, which she had insisted on making, they had been encouraged not to come again. Emily was sure now that this was Madame's doing, but part of her had secretly been glad not to have to go. Papa King could not speak, Rosamund had told her, and she had found the noises he made when she visited so frightening, and his tendency to cry without warning so embarrassing, that she had not known what to do or say.

Now Emily forced herself to approach the bed. Papa King looked far worse than he had done the last time Emily had seen him, and with a shock she realized what in her heart she should have known long ago. Papa King was dying. It might take days or weeks; it might even be months; but one way or another, he would not be with them for long. It seemed unthinkable, but somehow she and Rosamund, and Artemisia itself, would have to go on without him.

Emily climbed up on to the chair beside the bed and took Papa King's hand in her two small ones. This was her only chance; she had to tell him what was happening, for she might never see him again. Part of her still hoped against hope that, sick and dying as he was, Papa King would be able to help her. His strength of will and force of character had held everything together for so long that it was impossible to believe it was completely gone.

"It's Emily, Papa King," she said, in a soft urgent voice. The dark eyes opened, and Emily saw that the old Papa King was still there, hidden away inside the broken-down body on the bed. "Papa, I'm in terrible trouble, and you've got to help me. You sent Rosamund your key, didn't you? The key to the Most Secret Room? I don't know who helped you do it; perhaps it was your old secretary, Adelaide. But Madame didn't like it. She's been trying to kill Rose and me; she wants to be queen instead of Rose, and—" The door opened and Emily broke off. Standing in the doorway was Madame, and behind her, Ron Burton, the Minivers' former Chief of Security.

Emily dived off the chair and rolled under the bed. But Ron had already anticipated what she was going to do: he had trained both her and Rosamund in self-defence, and was there to catch her when she shot out the other side. A strong hand gripped her wrist. Emily felt something sharp in her arm. Her eyelids flickered and she went limp and slumped on the floor.

Ron stood up. He re-capped the syringe he had used to knock Emily out, and tossed it into a medical waste bin. On the bed behind them, Papa King was making strange agitated noises and trying helplessly to sit up.

Madame rounded on him. "Shut up!" she hissed. "Shut up, you stupid old man! Do you want Titus to hear?"

Ron gave her an odd look. "Titus is at the Archives," he said. "I don't think even he could hear from two blocks down the road."

"You never know what he's doing," said Madame darkly. "He's three steps ahead of you, at any rate."

Ron's face hardened. *And four steps ahead of you*, he

thought, but Madame was no longer looking at him. She was standing by Emily Miniver's unconscious form, and stirring it gently with her foot. For a moment, Ron thought she was going to kick her. With a shock, he realized that if that happened, he would have to do something. He had no particular liking for Emily: in fact, she and her sister had caused him a great deal of trouble. But the Minivers were scarcely bigger than babies. It was all right to overpower and even kidnap them, but there was a point where the line must be drawn.

"This isn't working," said Madame shortly, and at the expression on her face, Ron's qualms became stronger still. "Emily's only been here one day, and already she's tried to escape. We're going to have to do something. Keep her tied up and gagged, and hide her somewhere Titus won't find her. As soon as I've decided how to proceed, I'll let you know." She looked at Emily as if she was a parcel she had brought home from shopping and had somehow regretted purchasing – only Ron knew that Madame never went shopping, or did anything that cost her money if she could help it.

Ron popped Emily into a laundry hamper. He covered her with blankets, and wheeled the hamper out into the corridor. Madame started to follow, but a sound from the bed made her hesitate. She turned and went back to her father's side.

"You always thought you were so clever," she said. "When you sent me into exile with my mother, you never dreamed that I'd come back. You thought you'd replace me with the Minivers. Well, how does it feel now? Are you pleased with what you've done?"

Papa King made a noise in his throat. He stared up at his daughter, his dark eyes trying desperately to communicate. Madame refused to meet his gaze. Once, she had tried to kill Papa King. She did not want him to feel sorry for her now.

"Goodbye, Father," she said, and stalked out of the room. She did not look back, but behind her she could hear that Papa King was crying: for her, for Emily Miniver, and for himself, whose sins had brought them all to this pass.

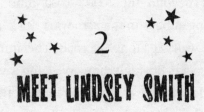

2
MEET LINDSEY SMITH

Down by the golf course, where the greens ended and a private roadway snaked along the riverbank, was a strip of mud and mangroves. It was a dank, smelly, secret kind of place. The mud, sharp roots and branches kept all but the keenest people from the water's edge. At dusk, a green mist seemed to hover over the river and the roadway, and the shadows swarmed with insects and smelled of decay.

Rosamund Miniver and her companion Livia Wallace huddled together under the shelter of a low-growing tree. Its branches made a kind of cave that was quite invisible from the road above, but the ground was wet, so they could not sit down properly even on the blanket they had brought with them. Rosamund was anxious, afraid and almost as hungry as the local mosquitoes. It was more than twenty-four hours since she and Livia had eaten a proper meal, but though they were both bone-achingly weary, they did not dare fall asleep.

Boats and jet skis roared along the river. Up on the

golf course beyond the road, Rosamund could hear golfers slicing at balls in the gathering dusk. A man with a dog came walking along the road. The animal, a black and white cocker spaniel, came lolloping towards them. It leaped down into the hollow where the tree was growing and snuffled enthusiastically over the ground.

"Star? Star, come back!"

Livia's fingers closed on Rosamund's arm and they shrank back against the tree. The dog continued to snuffle around their hiding place. Its friendly face burrowed under the branches until it saw Livia and Rosamund and began to bark. Livia froze at Rosamund's side. Rosamund picked up a stick and threw it.

"Shoo!" she hissed. "Go away!"

The dog barked even harder.

"Come on, Star!" called the owner sharply, and the spaniel turned reluctantly and ran back to the road.

Rosamund let out her breath. "That was close." She was scared of dogs at the best of times; they were too big and unpredictable for someone of her tiny size. Livia did not reply, and Rosamund began to feel annoyed. Since they had fled Miniver House, Livia had scarcely spoken to her. It was all very well to be upset, but Rosamund had spent her entire life enjoying other people's attention, and she did not appreciate being treated as if she did not exist.

10

"It's not my fault, you know," she said. "You don't have to treat me as if I smell."

Livia turned away. Her eyes welled with tears again, and Rosamund began to feel impatient. The problem was Livia's house. Her beautiful wooden cottage, with its yellow walls and a garden full of flowers, had been burned to the ground. Rosamund knew it had probably been Madame who had given the order to have the house destroyed. Rosamund was not surprised: it was just the sort of spiteful thing Madame would do. But Rosamund had not *wanted* it to happen. No one could say the loss of the house was her fault, it simply wasn't, and it wasn't fair of Livia to behave as if it somehow was.

They sat together a little longer, neither of them speaking a word to the other. The light continued to fade, and it had almost completely gone when Rosamund's sharp ears picked up the sound of a car with a powerful engine heading along the road. It was travelling at quite a speed, and as it rounded the bend close to where they were hiding, the driver applied the brakes and it came to a crunching halt. A door opened. Pleased to have an excuse to get away from Livia, Rosamund scrambled out of the bushes and looked up on to the road.

"Gibraltar?"

"Luckily for you, yes, it is," said a man, and at the

11

sound of his rich, familiar voice, Livia too emerged from undercover. Gibraltar reached down into the hollow and helped first Rosamund and then Livia out on to the road. He was a tall man with swarthy skin and eyes that always looked amused. Rosamund did not know much about him, apart from the fact that he wrote books and his real name was Peter Barnabas. She had always guessed there was much more to Gibraltar than he had told them, but despite the mystery surrounding him, she still trusted him more than any person she had ever met.

"Are you all right, Livia?" Gibraltar asked.

"Just tired." Livia turned to the four-wheel drive car that was waiting on the road, its engine running. Rosamund was already climbing into the cabin, hoping, against the odds, that Emily would be in the car. Of course she wasn't, for Emily would never have waited patiently if she had really been there, but as Rosamund pulled herself on to the floor of the passenger seat, she gave a cry of delight and recognition. A woman was sitting behind the wheel, a fat woman with frizzy ginger hair and a friendly smile. It was Lindsey Smith, the President and Founder of the Minivers Fan Club, the largest of the many Minivers clubs in Artemisia.

"Lindsey! How wonderful to see you!"

"Rose, my darling! You're safe!"

In three jumps, Rosamund had vaulted over the seat

and was being held in a smothering embrace. That Gibraltar had found Lindsey seemed like a miracle, for the club had largely turned against them, and she was now, Rosamund realized, probably one of the last true Minivers fans in existence. It made the fact of her being there doubly precious. When times were good and you were famous and popular, anybody could be a fan. It took a special type of person to stick by a former celebrity, whom the people with all the power were hunting down and whom the media were determined to destroy.

"Lindsey, you look so well!" said Rosamund warmly. "Are you feeling better?"

"Brilliant!" said Lindsey. "Well, not exactly brilliant. But quite well compared to last year, and even better for seeing you. Do you know, when you went missing, I lay in bed and cried for two days? Then some creepy woman from Miniver House Security came and took me away. She asked me all sorts of questions about where you might be. I didn't tell her anything, but I realized there was something up."

"There certainly has been," said Rosamund. "Did you hear my speech on the radio last night?"

Lindsey nodded vigorously. "Yes. It was brilliant! Do you know, the fans are talking about nothing else? There are pirate copies circulating all over Artemisia. But we can talk about that later. Hop in, you two," she called to Gibraltar and Livia, who were still standing on the road. "We don't want to hang around here any longer than we have to. Rose, you sit down there, on the floor, so you're out of sight."

Rosamund crouched down obediently in the passenger footwell. It was wonderful, after all that had happened, to find out that she and Emily still had fans, even if, as she suspected, they were mostly Lindsey's friends. Madame had worked very hard to ruin the Minivers' reputation, using reports in the newspapers and on television, and many people had turned against them as a result. Rosamund's radio broadcast had been made to try and win the fans back, but until this moment, she had scarcely wondered if anyone had even listened. The broadcast had led to Emily being captured by Madame. Rosamund could not help but blame herself for letting this happen.

Lindsey drove to the end of the narrow road, turned her Land Rover awkwardly around and drove off. As they headed out of the suburbs, the sun finished going down and it became properly dark. Rosamund could not see where they were going, but she talked to Lindsey as they drove along, asking after her family and other fans she remembered from the old days of the club. She did not mention Emily, and Lindsey, who was wiser than she sometimes appeared, knew better than to bring up the subject.

Sitting in the back seat, Gibraltar and Livia let them chatter on. Gibraltar listened without trying to join the conversation, but Livia had no interest in what Rosamund and Lindsey were saying. She stared out of the window, watching the streets and buildings flashing by, and tried to blank out her thoughts. Part of her still didn't believe what had happened. The smoking ruin of her house, with the fire engines parked in the street outside, could not have been real. Only it was real, and Livia knew with dreadful certainty that she could never go back. Her beautiful cottage was in ashes, along with all her books and paintings. All she had left was the dirty skirt and T-shirt she was wearing, a woven bag containing a sketchbook and twenty dollars, and a blanket from the boot of her car. Part of Livia thought she was going mad. Perhaps she *was* mad, and that was why her head felt the way it did . . . as if it was a giant pumpkin, about to explode. . .

Gibraltar laid a hand briefly on her shoulder. It did not mean anything: he was just being kind, but Livia felt something twist inside her. She bit her lip to stop from crying, but it did not work. The tears were trickling down her face yet again when the Land Rover turned unexpectedly off the main road and swayed and

15

bounced along a dirt track to a gate. Gibraltar got out of the car and opened it. A yellow light was shining up ahead among the trees.

"This is my aunt's place," Lindsey explained. "I've been living with her ever since I got sick, last year. It's all right: she knows you're coming. Aunt Edie's a Minivers fan, too."

She drove through the gate and the dirt gave way to a gravel driveway. A few minutes later they pulled up at the door of a house. It was built of dark brick, with a green door, and there was a chimney at one end of the roof. A flower bed at the entrance was full of topiary bushes, with daisies and white Sweet Alice, which seemed to glow in the evening gloom. It was so beautiful and so normal that, even in the midst of her anxiety over Emily, Rosamund felt comforted and finally began to relax.

The door opened and an elderly woman came out.

"Did you find them?" she cried, as Lindsey killed the engine. "Where are they?" The car doors began opening and everyone climbed out: Gibraltar and Livia, and finally, Rosamund. Aunt Edie stared at her in dismay and for a moment Rose saw herself as she must now appear: not the glamorous miniature celebrity that people were used to, but a filthy little creature smeared with mud and smelling of mangroves, her long hair hacked off savagely close to her head. Yet it was not Rosamund's appearance that had caused Aunt Edie to falter. She rounded on Lindsey and demanded, "But where's the other one? Where's Emily?"

Lindsey looked at her aunt in horror. It was too late. The name had finally been spoken and Rosamund burst into tears.

It was after hours at the City Archives, but lights were burning in the ground floor reception area. The space looked as if a bomb had gone off inside it. The reception desk had been tipped over and the telephone had been ripped from its socket. Filing cabinets had been emptied and the contents strewn across the floor. The room was filled with blue-shirted guards from the Minivers' former security team, who were closing off the building with ruthless efficiency. A few frightened-looking archivists in dustcoats stood huddled in a corner, watching as the room was pulled apart. Several of them were crying, but they had not put up any fight. They dared not, for the people from Operation Miniver were armed.

The big doors opened and a young man walked in. He was tall and fair, dressed in jeans and a black cotton shirt. Everything about him was completely nondescript, except for his face. It was covered with cuts and bruises as if he had been in a fight, and his swollen upper lip gave an unpleasant sneer to his expression. For a moment, the young man looked around the room, surveying the devastation with apparent satisfaction. When he had finished, he turned to a dark woman, not in uniform, who was overseeing the other guards.

"Holly, is everything secure?"

"Yes, Titus. No one can get in or out."

"Good work." Titus nodded, and Holly preened at the compliment. She was not part of Operation Miniver, but was a member of the Minivers Fan Club Committee, and had supported Titus when he had turned the club against Emily and Rosamund. Titus turned to the gathered staff, and addressed them.

"Ladies and gentlemen, as of this evening, I am replacing Ms Glenda Milton as City Archivist. Ms Milton has already been relieved of her position, and you are all dismissed without further notice. Any attempt to remove property from the building will result in your immediate arrest and prosecution. You there, trying to hide at the back, will stay behind." Titus pointed to a well-dressed man, and a guard seized him by the arm and dragged him away. "Throw the others out," said Titus and without further comment, he thrust his hands into his pockets and strode from the room.

Titus went up the main staircase, his long legs taking the steps two at a time. On the first floor was an imposing door marked *City Archivist*. It was closed, but the lock had already been forced. Titus kicked it open. The office beyond was ultra modern, with white carpet and walls covered with pictures of its former owner. Somewhere along the corridor a woman was shouting loudly. "You can't do this to me! I'm the City Archivist! I have a contract! Let me go!" Titus picked up an engraved paperweight that was sitting on the desk. The inscription read: *MANAGE, MODERNIZE AND MOVE ON*. Titus tossed the paperweight into the bin and pushed a buzzer.

"Have Ms Milton arrested and sent to the watch-house, will you, Holly? She is creating a nuisance. And show Mr McMahon up to my office. I want to talk to him."

"Right away, Titus."

When Holly arrived a minute later with the archivist who had been taken out of the group downstairs, Titus was sitting in Glenda Milton's chair. Tom McMahon was a young man with bad skin and slightly greasy hair, and clearly dressed in expensive clothes to make up for not being handsome. He looked extremely nervous and Titus, who made it his business to find out about most people crossing his path, knew that it was not just

19

because he had been singled out. Tom McMahon had been Assistant Archivist to Glenda Milton. Two days before, thinking he was being very clever, Tom had informed Madame that Titus was searching for a secret room. The Most Secret Room contained evidence of her attempt to murder her father, Papa King. Madame had ordered Ron Burton to arrest Titus, and he had been beaten up. Tom was now afraid that Titus knew what he had done, which of course, he did. That could wait, though. There was nothing Titus enjoyed more than waiting.

"Thank you, Holly, that's all for now. You may go," said Titus. Holly left the room, and he turned to Tom. "Sit down, Mr McMahon. I want to talk to you."

Tom McMahon pulled up an uncomfortable-looking chair. He sat down, lacing his fingers nervously together. "Of course, sir, if I can help in any way. . ."

"You can, and if you know what's good for you, you will," said Titus ominously. "I want all the information you can give me on the Most Secret Room."

"The Most Secret Room?" Tom stammered.

"Yes. Don't tell me you've never heard of it." Titus put his hand into his shirt and pulled out a small object that was dangling on a string. "It does exist. This is Papa King's key. The City Archivist has the other half, and I know for a fact the entrance is somewhere in this office."

Tom thought a moment. Titus guessed that he was wondering just how much he should say.

"Are you sure?" asked Tom.

"Oh yes. I'm sure. I was told by a man who helped to build it." Titus leaned back in his chair. "Glenda Milton says she knows nothing about it. Tell me, has this office always been in the same place?"

"I think so. Of course, Ms Milton had it extensively renovated. The design won a prize for interior decoration. The work cost nearly a hundred thousand dollars."

"What a pity," said Titus. "Because it's all got to go. I want this office taken apart, brick by brick, and you are going to help. Bring in workmen. Lift the floorboards, take the plaster off the walls. Report back to Holly, and do exactly as she tells you. I want the Most Secret Room found. Do you understand?"

"Yes, sir." Tom swallowed. "Is there anything else I can do for you, sir?"

"Yes," said Titus unexpectedly. "As a matter of fact, there is. You can tell me where you buy your suits."

When Tom had gone, Titus put a hand into his pocket and brought out a small address book. He laid the book on the glass desktop and looked approvingly around him. He had never had an office of his own before. Unlike most people, Titus did not care about money, or possessions, or being seen to be important. Given a choice, he preferred to put his plans into action behind the scenes, where other people were unaware of his schemes and would blame their evil results on someone else. But it would be useful to have a base just now, particularly one that was so close to the Most Secret Room.

Titus opened the address book. It contained the names of people Titus intended to get even with, and went back a very long way. A satisfyingly large number of names had been crossed out, but there was plenty of room for more. Titus flicked through the book until he reached the tab for M. He wrote Tom McMahon's name there in thick black letters, then paused and drew a circle around the names on the line above. Titus had not forgotten Rosamund and Emily Miniver. For them, he was willing to wait a very long time indeed.

3
EMILY IN DANGER

Ron Burton sat in his living room, looking down at Emily Miniver. She lay on the sofa, fast asleep, and her pale skin, mop of glossy dark hair and slightly turned-up nose reminded him inexplicably of a kitten. Emily had been asleep all day. She had started to wake up twice from the injection Ron had given her at the palace, but before she had come around properly, he had made her unconscious again. Now Ron was a little concerned that he had given her too much of the drug. Emily had been out for at least an hour longer than with the previous doses. Minivers were not built like normal-sized people, and it was hard to judge the proper amount to give to someone so small.

Ron did not want to harm Emily. It was true that he had betrayed her to Madame, but though he was a hard man, he was not cruel, and he had done the things he had for a good reason. For many years, Ron had been the Miniver sisters' Chief of Security. He had worked long hours, making sure that Emily and Rosamund stayed safe, whether at home or at public events when they appeared before their fans. Ron had always been well paid, but the work was demanding and often dull, and he had never earned quite enough to feel satisfied. Even this had been bearable; but then something terrible had happened that had changed Ron's outlook on everything. Ron's only son, Alex, had been hit by a car. His one chance of walking again was an expensive operation, and Ron and his wife, Sandra, did not have the money to pay for it.

Alex was in hospital right now. The money for the operation had eventually come from Madame, who had paid it to Ron in return for betraying the Minivers. The doctors had told Ron and Sandra that everything was going well. But with the danger of the surgery over, Ron found himself beginning to worry about other things. To begin with, he did not like having Emily Miniver in his house. She and Rosamund were Artemisia's most wanted fugitives, and the longer she stayed there, sleeping on his sofa, the greater the risk that she would be discovered. If that happened, Ron knew that Madame would have no hesitation in letting him take all the blame: her position was shaky, and she was extremely good at running away from trouble. But it was not Madame that Ron was worrying about. It was Titus.

24

The telephone rang in the kitchen. Ron went through and picked it up.

"Hello, Sandra. How's Alex this afternoon?"

Sandra gave him the latest report from the doctor. It seemed that everything was going well, and there was even talk of letting Alex sit up. But the patient was restless. "He wants to see his dad, Ron," said Sandra. "When are you coming up to the hospital?"

"Er – I can't make it just now," said Ron, glancing through the doorway at the unconscious Emily. "I'm really sorry, Sandra. You know how things are at the moment. Put Alex on and I'll talk to him."

"All right," said Sandra, but she did not sound happy. There was a pause as the phone was handed over and a boy's weak voice piped up on the other end of the line.

"Dad?"

"Hi, Alex," said Ron. A lump came into his throat and he cleared it with a self-conscious cough. "How are you going, son?"

"Not bad," Alex replied. "It still hurts, but they give me needles all the time. Grandma visited this morning. She brought me some chocolates and a copy of *Flying* magazine. Guess what? I can wriggle my toes."

"That's great," said Ron. "Tremendous. You'll be up and walking in no time."

"Maybe," said Alex. "Dad, there's something else. Do

you know a man with blond hair and bruises on his face? He came in this morning after Grandma. He said he was a friend of yours, and that I should let you know he'd visited. Dad? Dad, are you still there?"

"I'm here." Ron's mind was whirring like a computer. "Alex, are you listening? I want you to pay careful attention to what I'm saying. That man is not a friend of mine. If he comes back, you are not to speak to him, do you understand? Tell him to leave, and call hospital security if you have to. Now put your mother on: I need to talk to her."

Ron spoke briefly to Sandra, gave her some instructions about what to do if Titus returned, then hung up. For a moment he stood by the telephone. He felt badly rattled, which of course was what Titus had intended. Alex and Sandra meant the world to him. Everything Ron had done, he had done for them, and Titus would not forget this. Nor would he forget that two days before, on Madame's orders, Ron had taken him prisoner and punched him in the face. Ron knew that very soon Titus would be back for his revenge.

Ron had first met Titus when he was vice-president of the Minivers Fan Club. He had been very polite and helpful, and at that stage, had tended to stay in the background. Ron had not really paid him much attention, and he had been quite surprised to discover that Titus, too, was working with Madame to bring down the Minivers. Ron had never quite understood why Titus was doing this, but he had learned enough to realize that his motives were entirely sinister. Now, Titus was holed up in the City Archives, and most of Ron's old security team were with him. They were part of Operation Miniver now, and many of the guards were beginning to look to Titus for their orders instead of him. Ron knew that was the way Titus worked. He had started off being so pleasant that it was hard to believe he had anything evil in mind at all. Then, little by little, he revealed his true nature. Titus was treacherous, cold-hearted and very dangerous, and Ron was honest enough to admit that Titus was also far cleverer than he was.

A small noise, like a footstep, made Ron look around. Emily Miniver was standing in the doorway between the kitchen and the lounge room, looking white and ill. Ron was reminded of the time she and Rosamund both had flu, and he had carried them out into the garden so they could sit in the sun. The memory was an uncomfortable one, and he spoke in a voice that was unexpectedly harsh.

"You're awake."

Emily nodded cautiously. "Can— Can I have a drink of water?"

"If you want one." Ron stepped back and Emily came into the kitchen. Of course, she could not reach the tap, but Ron was surprised to note that she did not ask him to help her. Moving carefully, for she was still groggy, Emily pushed a chair over to the sink, climbed up on to it, and found a clean glass on the drainer. She filled it with water and drank thirstily, watching Ron through the corner of her eye as she did so. When she had finished, Emily rinsed the glass, put it back on the drainer and turned to face him.

"Where are we?"

"This is my house."

"Your house?" Emily looked surprised. "Why am I here?"

"That's really none of your business, Emily." Ron gestured to the kitchen floor, indicating that she should get off the chair. But Emily did not climb down. She stayed standing where she was, looking Ron squarely in the face, until he began to feel extremely awkward. When the telephone rang a second time, he was glad to have the excuse to answer it.

"Ron Burton speaking."

"It's Titus," said a woman's voice. There was no other introduction, but Ron knew at once the caller was Madame. "He's just been to see me. He told me I must call the Parliament."

Ron clutched the receiver. "But—" He looked at Emily, who was still watching from the chair, and forced himself to keep his expression calm. "Have you done what he's asked?"

"Not yet," said Madame. "I don't have any choice, though. If I disobey, Titus says he has ways of making me do whatever he wants." Her voice cracked in terror. "It's years since Parliament last did any real business. Half the MPs are dead and the others are so old they might as well be. Titus is making me fill all the vacant seats with the members of the Minivers Fan Club Committee. He's giving one to Len, Holly, even that stupid Brenda Bertram. But he hasn't given one to you, Ron. Your name isn't on the list, and I daren't put it on. Titus is out to get you, the same way he's out to get me. Do you understand?"

"Yes," said Ron. His mouth was dry. "I understand."

"Good," said Madame. "We have to work together, Ron. Don't forget I gave you that hundred thousand dollars. I could ask for it back, you know, any time."

"That was a gift," said Ron.

"It was a bribe," said Madame coldly, "and don't you forget it. We need to move quickly. The first thing to do is get rid of Emily. She's no use to us now, and if she escapes again it could be fatal. I've ordered Primrose to help you. Dispose of her carefully, and when you've done

29

the job, come to me for further instructions." There was a click as she hung up and Ron was left holding the receiver and staring at Emily Miniver.

For almost the first time in his life, he was afraid.

In her bedroom in the Artemisia Palace, Madame replaced her own receiver with a trembling hand. Her stomach was churning so badly she felt like she was going to be sick. Madame was not disturbed because she had ordered Ron to murder Emily Miniver. Emily was in her way and had to be got rid of, it was as simple as that. But while Madame was good at telling lies about herself, when it came to self-preservation, she could be surprisingly honest. Ordering Emily's death was a measure of how desperate things really were. It was a sign that her arch-enemy, Titus, was now almost completely in control.

Over the last few days Madame had been under a great deal of pressure. Until now, she had mostly enjoyed her time in the spotlight, and though her schemes had not always gone according to plan, she had been confident Ron and Titus had things under control. But from the moment Titus had told her he knew the location of the Most Secret Room, and that she must do exactly as he ordered, Madame had not had a moment's peace. At times, she felt so paralysed by terror that she had come close to packing up her things and running away. The only thing that stopped her doing it was the knowledge that she would be abandoning all hope of becoming queen. Madame had already been banished from Artemisia once. If she left the city this time, she knew it would be for ever.

Madame pictured Titus in some hidden basement in the City Archives, opening a concealed door and entering the Most Secret Room. She saw his eyes greedily devouring the shameful story of her disgrace and banishment, and she hugged her arms tightly to her chest. How dare he? How dare Titus enter a private room, built by her grandmother; a place where secrets might be kept from the rest of the world? Just the thought of him poring over her family papers was like finding a slug in her salad. Worst of all, if Titus discovered the contents of Papa King's will. . .

Papa King. Always, everything came back to Papa King. Madame thought of her father, lying in his bed downstairs, and with a little jolt, she remembered something important. The key to the Most Secret Room had been made in two pieces, one for the King or Queen of Artemisia, and one for the City Archivist. Titus had stolen Papa King's half from the Minivers, but the City

Archivist's key was lost. All that was left of it was a wax imprint, made many years before by her mother.

Madame opened the drawer to her bedside table. It was crammed with threadbare hankies and old ends of lipsticks that she was too mean to throw away; bits of string and elastic bands she had saved; and a photograph of her mother on which she had once drawn a moustache and which she was now too embarrassed to keep in its frame. Madame burrowed through the rubbish to the back of the drawer and there, at the very back, was the tiny tin containing the key print. All through their hateful exile, her mother had kept it safe. But leaving the print in the drawer now was to risk Titus getting hold of it. She had to find a hiding place, but where? Madame tapped her fingers impatiently on the tin. As she did so, her cat, Kitty, came crawling out from underneath a chair and mewed.

"Here, Kitty. Come here, sweetheart; come to Mother." Madame went down on her haunches and beckoned. Kitty came forward suspiciously. She was hoping for extra food, which was never very likely, since Madame was economical with cat biscuits and everyone else in the palace heartily disliked her. Madame grabbed Kitty and unbuckled her collar. It was strong enough for Madame to attach the little tin to, and when she had covered the collar over with a faded blue ribbon that she had saved from a parcel, it was almost completely invisible.

"Good girl, Kitty. Good girl." Madame chucked her darling under the chin. She reached for the packet of cat biscuits she had stashed in a cupboard, and a few minutes later, Kitty was enjoying an unexpected treat. Never mind the waste, Madame told herself. Kitty had earned it. In a world that had always been against her, there was, quite literally, no one else she could trust.

4
MURDER IN THE DARK

Emily knew for certain something was up. She had been aware of it ever since Ron received the phone call, because although she had distinctly heard Madame's voice, he had pretended the call was from someone else. Emily had also caught the expression of shock on his face. Ron was normally good at covering up his thoughts, but something had been said to him that was so dreadful and unexpected that he could not hide his dismay. Emily was no fool, and she knew that it had to concern her.

In the weeks that she'd been on the run, Emily had developed a sixth sense for danger. Many times, she had found a way to wriggle out of a tricky situation, and she had survived several brushes with death. This time, though, things were different. Ron had been the Minivers' Chief of Security for nine years: he knew her intimately, and was taking no chances that she would outwit him. After his phone call, he fed Emily an apple and a sandwich, and left her sitting tied up in an armchair. Since Ron knew what he was doing, his knots were too tight for Emily to have any chance of slipping free.

There was a feeling in the air, like the electrical build-up before a thunderstorm. Emily did not understand what was happening, but she did know that unless something unexpected occurred to save her, she was in desperate trouble. The afternoon seeped slowly away, and there were several more phone calls. At first Emily thought Ron must be speaking to Madame, but after a while, she realized that he was calling someone at the Artemisia Hospital. It transpired that Ron's son, Alex, had just had an operation, that he was lonely and in pain, and that he badly wanted his father to visit.

"I'm sorry, Alex," said Ron. "I can't come now. I've already explained I've got to work. No, I won't be up this evening. There's something I've got to do." He glanced at Emily as he said this, and looked away. Emily dropped her eyes. She had never even met Alex Burton, but she knew perfectly well it was because of him that she was here now.

The Minivers could have paid for Alex's operation quite easily. The fact was, as Emily now uncomfortably realized, it had never occurred to her and Rosamund that Ron and his family might need their help. They had been too bound up in their careers as miniature superstars to give Alex Burton more than a moment's thought. If Ron had asked for money, they would certainly have given it, but Ron was not that sort of man. Instead, he had simply hidden away his feelings, growing more and more angry and resentful. Finally, someone else had offered him the money his family needed, and he had taken it. Emily was not entirely sure that she blamed him. She and Rosamund had been accused of many things; of being greedy, untalented and vain. But while most of the evil stories their enemies had spread about them in the newspapers and on television were lies and exaggeration told to destroy their reputation, the claim that they had done nothing for Alex Burton was true.

Emily could not help thinking that this mistake had brought down a heavy punishment, but there was nothing she could do to change things. As the afternoon gave way to evening, she became hungry and thirsty again, but this time there was no suggestion of anything to eat, and she did not ask for it. At last, at around ten o'clock, a car pulled up in the driveway. Emily heard someone get out, but whoever it was did not come into the house. Instead, Ron went outside. Emily could hear him, talking in the driveway, but she could not make out the conversation, and she did not know who Ron was with.

Emily twisted and wriggled her way to the edge of the

chair and jumped off. She could not walk with her legs tied together, but she hopped over to the window and looked out from behind the curtains. It was dark outside, which made it hard to see what was happening, but she could just make out a white van parked in the driveway. The driver's door was open, and beside it, talking to Ron, was a woman Emily recognized. She was Primrose McLennan, a former guard in the Miniver House Security Team and now the most brutal and unsympathetic member of Operation Miniver.

Primrose was not wearing her uniform. She was dressed in a dark T-shirt and work trousers, with her hair scraped up in a messy bun and a pair of down-at-heel wellingtons on her feet. It was the wellies that caught Emily's attention. She had never seen Primrose wearing them before and there was something funny about the way she kept shrugging her shoulders, as if they were stiff and sore. It was a familiar gesture, and Emily frowned, trying to remember what it reminded her of. What on earth could Primrose have been up to at this time of night? Then it struck her. It was the same shrug of pain that the Miniver House gardener had made, when he had spent an afternoon digging holes to plant the bushes for their new rose garden.

The idea that Primrose might have been digging holes too, was so frightening that Emily froze in terror. Then her senses returned, and a desperate urge to save herself took over. Ron had bound her wrists and ankles too efficiently to have left her any chance of escape, and there was no point in struggling with her bonds. Emily starting hopping in tiny jumps towards the door, but without the use of her arms she immediately lost balance and fell over. She could not get up again, so instead she started wriggling like a caterpillar across the carpet. Emily had barely made it to the coffee table when the front door opened and Ron came back into the room.

Emily stopped. Ron was carrying a small plastic box and a tiny bottle. Both these items were familiar to Emily, but the expression on Ron's face was not. Normally, Ron never showed what he was feeling or thinking. It was this that made him so dangerous. He had kidnapped Rosamund and never so much as blinked; he had plotted with Titus and started Operation Miniver, and no one, least of all Emily and Rosamund, had ever been any the wiser. But tonight Ron's face was a curious colour, a sort of greyish white, and there was knowledge in his eyes that he could not hide. He looked afraid. Suddenly, Emily knew what was going to happen. She was going to be drugged again, just like before; only this time she was not going to wake up.

She was going to die.

Ron stood holding the bottle in one hand and the box

containing the syringe in the other. He could see from Emily's expression that she knew what he meant to do, and that she was trying very hard not to let him see she was frightened. It did not make things easier for him. Ron knew he should have acted before this. All afternoon, he had been dreading this moment, putting it off while he pondered Madame's order and tried to work out what he should do.

Though Emily did not mean much to him, Ron was not a cold-blooded poisoner. If it had not been for Alex, he would never have found himself in this situation, and he knew it. Now Alex had undergone his operation there was nothing whatever to gain from obeying Madame. What he needed now was protection for Alex and Sandra from Titus, and Ron did not think for a moment that Madame could offer them that.

Ron turned back to Emily. She was still gazing at him, and she looked small and terrified. Ron took an uncertain step forwards, and then he remembered Primrose. She was still waiting outside. Ron knew she had her eye on his job. If he failed now, she would be waiting to tell Madame all about it.

Ron straightened his back. He took a handkerchief from his pocket and advanced towards Emily. . .

Out on the driveway, Primrose was waiting impatiently by the van. It was a white tradesman's vehicle, like hundreds of others on the road, and the number plates had been carefully changed to confuse anybody who might notice them. Primrose was tired. She had already driven the van out to the local forest and worked hard all afternoon getting everything ready for Ron. She had come back, expecting to find he had already finished the job. *Why on earth was it taking him so long?* thought Primrose, crossly. Surely it couldn't be *that* hard. After all, it wasn't as though he cared for the little beast. . .

A thin high scream sounded inside the house and was abruptly cut off. Primrose was suddenly glad she had stayed with the van. Several minutes passed, during which her stomach churned with fear, and at last the front door opened. Ron came out, carrying a cardboard box. It was obviously heavy and the bottom bulged slightly under the weight of its contents.

Primrose hurried to open the sliding door on the side of the van. Ron set the box down carefully on the metal floor and pushed it in. It was smaller than Primrose had expected, and she had to remind herself that Emily was not very large.

Primrose tried to sound casual. "Any problems?"

"None," said Ron, shortly. He looked drawn and pale and Primrose was surprised. She had always thought

Ron was tough. She closed the van door with a hollow clunk and the two of them climbed into the cab. Primrose started the engine, and the van rolled out of the driveway and headed off down the street.

They drove swiftly and without conversation towards the outskirts of the city. Primrose turned off on to an obscure side road, and they struck out along a dirt track. It led to an isolated spot in the forest, and it was so dark Primrose had to use the odometer on the van to find it again. When they reached the proper place, she got out and led Ron by torchlight to the hole she had dug earlier in the day. Primrose had put it between two large trees, and because of the roots, and the fact that she was working alone, it was not particularly deep.

"That's awfully shallow," said Ron, disapprovingly. "We don't want foxes digging up the box." Primrose's aching shoulders slumped at the thought of more work, but luckily Ron seemed as anxious as she was to get the business over with. He jumped down into the hole and lifted down the box, and Primrose started to shovel in the dirt around it. The sound of the earth rattling on the cardboard was rather creepy. An unwanted image flashed into Primrose's head: of Emily as she had seen her just a month before, being fitted for a green sequinned party frock. She was standing, smiling, on a small catwalk in the designer's studio, while Rosamund sat on the

41

workbench swinging her legs and offering enthusiastic comments. Primrose was not an imaginative woman, but the memory made her shiver. She was glad when the hole was filled and the box had disappeared.

"That'll do," said Ron. They firmed down the earth with their boots and scattered leaves and stones over the top to hide the freshly turned earth. As they got back into the van and drove away, Primrose glanced curiously across at Ron. It seemed to her that, compared to his nervous manner on the way out, he was now unusually relaxed. He did not look at all like a man who had just committed a murder, which, if she had only known the truth, was not surprising.

The box they had just buried in the forest was full of old bath towels and seventeen paperback books.

Alex Burton wanted to be an airline pilot. His bookcase was stuffed with books and videos about planes. Models of fighter aircraft hung from his ceiling on fishing line. There were posters of jets and helicopters on the walls, and a half-completed plastic kit of a Short Stirling bomber sat on his desk where he had been working on it before he went to hospital. It was as if, stuck in his wheelchair, Alex had dreamed of escaping, of soaring beyond the confines of his lonely bedroom. Emily lay in the dark looking at the jumble of books and magazines on the bedside table, and wished she could fly away herself.

Emily was very scared. Earlier, she had been convinced that Ron was going to murder her, but instead, he had unexpectedly put away the syringe and gagged her with his handkerchief. Then he had hidden her in Alex's bedroom and driven off, taking with him a great armful of pocket aircraft guides from Alex's bookcase. Emily did not know what to make of this. She had not trusted Ron from the moment she had discovered he was working for Operation Miniver, but if he was truly on Madame's side, there seemed to be no explanation for what he was doing.

It was after two o'clock when Emily finally heard the sound of the returning van. The house door opened, lights were switched on in the corridor, and the bedroom door opened. Ron appeared in the doorway, a sharp-looking pocketknife in his hand.

Emily wanted to cry, but she was too proud to let Ron know she was frightened. She thought of Millamant, who had looked after her and Rosamund, and how she would want her to be brave. It was not as if she had never faced death before. Emily might just as easily have died when she had fallen from the Big Wheel at the

Artemisia Funfair, or when she had been swept away by rapids during their escape from the forest. For weeks she and Rosamund had been living with the odds stacked against them. Only Emily had never thought that when death came, it would be at the hands of Ron, whom she had known since she was a baby. Ron was not like Titus, or even Madame. He had looked after her and Rosamund for so long that, in a funny way, he was family.

Ron swung his knife towards her and stooped. Emily winced and closed her eyes, and then she felt the cords that tied her wrists unexpectedly break free. Ron's hand reached briefly behind her head and the gag went slack in her mouth.

"Oh." Emily felt her bruised wrists, and looked up at him uncomprehendingly.

"I've been a complete fool," said Ron. "It may be too late to fix things: I don't know. But if you'll help me, and work with me, we might be able to do something about this mess. Can you trust me, Emily? Can you forgive me?"

There was only one answer Emily could give. "Yes," she said. "Yes, of course, I can."

5

AT AUNT EDIE'S

When Rosamund woke around three o'clock, rain was falling, and obviously had been for some time. It streamed in dreary grey sheets from the eaves of the house, drenching the garden and driveway outside her window. The darkened room was unfamiliar and she felt a stab of fear at finding herself alone again. Her weariness had not carried her through the night. Now she was awake, she knew that she would not be able to go back to sleep.

Rosamund pushed back the bedding and stood up on the sofa. Through Aunt Edie's living-room curtains she could make out the shadow of the garage and the clipped shapes of the topiary bushes along the drive. The white daisies had gone to sleep, and the bushes were bent with rain. There was no sign of Lindsey's Land Rover, for Gibraltar had borrowed it. He had gone into the city to see what he could discover about Emily, and it was obvious he had not yet come back.

Rosamund had great faith in Gibraltar. She had first met him, by chance it seemed, when she had been kidnapped by the treacherous members of the Minivers Fan Club Committee. Gibraltar had saved Rosamund's life, and since then he had been a sure guide through her many troubles. But tonight even her firm faith in Gibraltar's ability to find a solution for every problem was wavering. An image kept replaying through her head like a damaged video recording: the ghastly moment when Gibraltar's caravan, in which Rosamund herself had ordered Emily to stay, had been towed through the gates of the Artemisia Palace to the waiting Madame. Rosamund knew Emily was resourceful and brave; far braver, in fact, than she was herself. But even the bravest people sometimes find themselves in situations they cannot escape from, and the wait for news of her sister was almost driving Rosamund mad.

There was nothing to see outside. Rosamund turned impatiently away from the window, and switched on a lamp that stood on a side table. Aunt Edie's living room was full of beautiful things, including a piano and an antique Chinese cabinet, but Rosamund was more interested in the television, which at least offered the prospect of something to do. She turned it on and started flicking through the channels. Not surprisingly,

46

there were no shows worth watching, but there was a video player on the shelf below. Prompted by some destructive impulse, Rosamund flicked the channel to the AV channel and pressed the play button.

The machine whirred for a moment and all at once there they were: Emily and herself, the miniature stars of *The Minivers' Music Hour*, sashaying in perfect time across the screen. They were dressed in dark-pink skirts with beaded fringes that swung and caught the light. Rosamund remembered the day they had recorded that segment in front of a packed studio audience: how Emily had tripped over a cable before they went on set, and skinned her knee, and how they had taped the graze and sprayed it with make-up so it wouldn't show. It must have hurt horribly, but there was no hint of pain on Emily's face as she stepped into the spotlight and sang her verse of their song. Abruptly, Rosamund hit the pause button, and the picture froze on the screen: Emily in close-up, oblivious to the coming disaster. Even the tiny beads of sweat on Emily's forehead seemed to glow with life and happiness. As she had done so many times in the last dreadful weeks, Rosamund broke down and started to cry.

"Stop it! You idiot, stop it!" Rosamund told herself fiercely, but the words had no effect and the tears kept coming. If Emily really was dead, she thought, she might as well give herself up to Madame. There would be no point at all in being alive.

The living-room door opened. Rosamund wiped her eyes hastily and looked up. Lindsey was standing in the doorway, her large comfortable figure swathed in a pink tent of a nightgown.

"Rose? Are you all right?"

"I'm fine," said Rosamund. She forced herself to smile. "I couldn't sleep. I thought I'd wait up for Gibraltar."

"Hmm," said Lindsey. "It's too early for him, I'd say. It's only three o'clock. Why don't I make us some tea?" She passed through into the kitchen and Rosamund scrubbed her eyes on her pillow, grateful to have the chance to compose herself. By the time Lindsey came back with the tea tray, she was sitting quietly on the sofa, only her red-rimmed eyes betraying her outburst.

Lindsey put the tray on the coffee table and sat down, the sofa sinking under her bulk. She nodded at the television. "That's 'Changing Places', isn't it? You did such a good job of that song. I was there that night, when you recorded it."

"I remember," said Rosamund. "It was just before Papa King had his stroke. Look. You can see him in the audience." She fast-forwarded the picture on quickly from the close-up of Emily and froze it again on Papa King, sitting proudly at the front in his special chair.

48

Rosamund stared at the picture for a moment, then pumped the zoom button. "My goodness. Will you look at that?"

"What is it?"

"It's Titus. Look, he's there, just behind Papa King. I never knew he was in the audience that night. I always thought he must have come to Artemisia with Madame. Do you think he was planning something even then?"

Lindsey produced a pair of glasses. She put them on and inspected the picture. "Not a doubt about it," she said. "Titus has always been up to no good. I don't know what he is doing, but I'm certain he's not working for Madame. I think he's really working for himself."

"I still don't know who Titus really is," said Rosamund. "I'm not even sure if he's from Artemisia."

"Oh, Titus is Artemisian all right," said Lindsey. "I do know that much. He told me once that his father worked at the Artemisia Hospital, but the family left many years ago, and I'm not sure if his parents are still alive. Apart from that, all I know is that he arrived out of the blue one day, and before I knew it he was practically running my club. The moment he got on to the Minivers Fan Club Committee, everything changed for the worse."

"How?" Rosamund asked.

Lindsey shrugged. "Well, he was very quiet, but he kept doing things behind my back. He took over the merchandising section and the sales went right down: I'm pretty sure he was stealing the money. And he used to write articles for the newsletters that gave me the creeps. They were supposed to be about how wonderful you were, but they always left you feeling there was something wrong with being a Minivers fan. There was one I actually stopped him from publishing. We had a huge row about it, and it was just after we quarrelled that I first got sick. The doctors never got to the bottom of what was wrong with me, but I don't think I was sick at all. I think I was poisoned."

"Poisoned?" Rosamund was shocked. "Lindsey, you might have been killed!"

"If I hadn't left the city, I probably would have been," said Lindsey. "Titus is a very frightening person, Rose. I always knew he wasn't really a fan. He used to talk about you and Emily as if he was, but there was no love in his voice. I don't think Titus cares about anybody but himself."

Rosamund was silent. Until quite recently, it had never occurred to her that a fan might be anything but friendly. Of course, there were a few nutty ones, but most of them were ordinary Artemisians, who had grown up loving the Minivers and what they stood for.

Now it seemed that the simple fact of being a Miniver, or even a fan of the Minivers, had taken on a dark and dreadful aspect that was beyond her power to comprehend.

"I sometimes wonder if there are any true fans left," she said.

"Of course there are," said Lindsey. "The club is scattered, and a lot of the members have dropped away, but people haven't stopped loving the Minivers. They'll come back, you'll see. That broadcast of yours *did* make a difference. People listened to it, and they're still listening to it. The members who were at the heart of the club haven't drifted away."

"The others have," said Rosamund, in a tiny voice.

Lindsey took her hand. "Did I ever tell you," she said, "about how I started the club? When they found you in that shoebox on the hospital steps, I was unemployed. Nobody would give me a job. I had no money, and nothing to do. Then I saw you in the newspaper, and I thought there was someone lonelier and more abandoned than myself. I started cutting out the articles. I cut out so many that in the end the *Artemisia Mail* published a story about me. Fourteen people wrote in, and that was how the Minivers Fan Club started. Fourteen people: that was all it took. The club grew from nothing. I know we can do it again."

"But what's the point?" said Rosamund. "You can't seriously think that all this," she gestured to the television, "is ever going to come back. Besides, without Emily, the Minivers are finished. I'm so afraid, Lindsey. I keep wondering whether we'll ever find Emily again. If she's gone for good, if she's – dead – I might as well give up now."

"Of course Emily isn't dead," said Lindsey. "To destroy the Minivers, Madame and Titus need you both. They might use Emily as a hostage or as bait to lure you into a trap, but they'll never kill her while you're still free. Your best way of saving Emily is to survive. Do what Papa King intended when he gave you that key Gibraltar told me about. You must become Queen of Artemisia."

"Everyone keeps saying that," said Rosamund despairingly. "I've tried to think of myself as queen, and I just can't. Anyway, Papa King is still alive. Until I hear he's dead, I won't even consider it."

"I understand why you feel like that," said Lindsey. "But the fact is, Rose, unless you do something now, when Papa King does die you won't get the chance. Think of it as your destiny, and don't fight it."

"If it's my destiny it will happen anyway," said Rosamund firmly. "I wouldn't know where to begin, and without Emily I don't intend to try." She turned off the TV with its frozen picture of Titus, and looked out again at the rain-soaked garden. "I do wish Gibraltar would come back. He'd know what I should do, and at least when he's around, Livia doesn't behave quite so strangely. I know she never liked me, but I always thought she was on our side. Now I'm not even sure about that. I know it's mean of me, but it would be so much easier without her." A small creak sounded out in the hall as she said this. Rosamund looked up, but the noise was not repeated, and she thought no more about it.

"I wouldn't worry about Livia," Lindsey said. "The poor girl's in shock. Don't forget, she's just lost her home."

"I know, and I'm very sorry for her," said Rosamund. "But I've lost my home, too. I'd burn Miniver House to the ground if I thought it would bring back Emmie. Maybe Livia needs to realize that some things are more important than houses."

Her words floated out into the hallway, where Livia was leaning against the newel post at the bottom of the staircase. She had not meant to eavesdrop. Lindsey's footsteps had woken her up, and she had come downstairs for a drink, reaching the hall just as the conversation turned to her. Now, Livia could not make up her mind whether to go or stay. That Rosamund should speak like this did not surprise her. She had always known that she was being taken for granted, but it was particularly ugly to have to listen to it being said out loud.

Against her will, Livia's eyes welled with tears. From the moment Rosamund had arrived on the steps of the Artemisia Hospital in that famous shoebox, she had been spoiled and selfish. Livia had never liked her, but she had done her best for her, because she thought Rosamund had been treated badly. Livia had lost her job, her car, her home and everything it contained because of the Minivers. How much more did Rosamund want? How much longer would she continue to behave like some kind of star, around whom the rest of the world was supposed to revolve? The thought of Rosamund ever becoming Queen of Artemisia turned Livia's grief to burning anger. Her hand strayed to the neck of her borrowed nightgown, and gripped a tiny object hanging around her neck.

Over my dead body, Livia thought. And clutching the half-key to the Most Secret Room that had belonged to her grandfather the City Archivist, she turned and fled back up the stairs.

Around the time that these thoughts were going through Livia's head, Gibraltar was pulling up outside the burned house in Daventry Street. There was not much left to see of it. The people who had set it on fire had been thorough, and the little wooden cottage had flared up as fiercely as if it had been made of paper. As Gibraltar parked Lindsey's Land Rover a little way along the street, the charred remains were still smoking faintly in the drizzle that hung in the air.

Gibraltar was trying to find out what had happened to Emily. So far, he had not had much success, but from the little he had managed to learn, he held grave fears for her safety. Two nights before, he, Rosamund and Livia had seen the caravan from which Emily had been coordinating the Radio Free Minivers operation being towed through the gates of the Artemisia Palace. Neither the van, nor the man who had stolen it, had been seen since. The Palace had gone into a curious sort of lockdown, and Titus had moved to the City Archives. Gibraltar, who knew more about Titus than he had let on to the others, had his own suspicions about why he had come to Artemisia so determined to wreak ruin on the Minivers; and he did not like the sound of this at all. But for now he had to concentrate on the job he was doing. If Emily had somehow managed to escape, Gibraltar knew that this was where she would have come.

He got out of the car. It was raining, not very heavily, but enough to make it uncomfortably wet for someone who did not have an umbrella. Gibraltar hunched his shoulders against the drizzle and walked up to Livia's charred and ruined front fence. The fire service had tied a reflective tape across the driveway. Gibraltar snapped the tape with one hand and carefully stepped through into what was left of the garden.

Only a few days before it had been lush and beautiful, but now the trees were burned to skeletons, and there was nothing underfoot but mud and ash. Gibraltar stood in the shadows and surveyed the scene. The site appeared to be deserted, but there was a strange watchful prickling in the back of his neck, and as he picked his way down what was left of the path at the side of the house, he felt sure someone was watching him. The space under the house was still wet from the fire service's hoses, and the house creaked and swayed on its stumps like a dying creature. Surely whoever else was here could not be reckless enough to be hiding in there. . .

"Emily?" Gibraltar ducked carefully under the back steps into the space under the house that had once been Livia's garage. The blaze had been so fierce that the ground beneath his boots was still warm, and little wisps of steam rose up in the cool night air. "Emily. Are you there?"

There was silence. It was so dark that Gibraltar could scarcely see, but though he had brought a torch he was reluctant to turn it on in case it attracted attention.

56

Suddenly something moved in the room above his head. There was a loud creak of charred floorboards, and ash and cinders showered down, as if someone moving above had disturbed some delicate balance. Gibraltar was not easily scared, but he knew that the house could collapse at any moment. He retreated quickly, and had almost reached the place where he had come in when there was a groaning, splintering, rending sound, and a section of burned-out floor fell crashing to the ground behind him.

A girl screamed. Gibraltar instantly snapped on his torch. He swept it over the wet and blackened timber above his head, and a small white face appeared in the gap in the floorboards, plainly terrified. It was not Emily Miniver, but a normal-sized girl of about her age. Gibraltar recognized her immediately as Fiona Bertram, the young fan whose mother, Brenda, was on Titus's committee, and who had helped them seize control of Radio Artemisia.

"Fiona!" Gibraltar called her name as loudly as he dared. "What are you doing here? How did you escape from the radio station? We all thought you must have been taken prisoner."

"They didn't find me," said Fiona. "I hid in a cupboard, and after everyone left, I came here looking for all of you. I thought there might be someone in the house, but the steps broke when I came up, and now the whole floor's given way and I can't get out!"

Gibraltar glanced over his shoulder at the back steps. There was no way he could use them; if they had crumbled under Fiona's weight, somebody his size would just go straight through. For Fiona to have got as far into the building as she had, she must have been amazingly desperate and brave. Gibraltar thought fast. The floor was clearly about to give way. When it did, it was likely to bring half the house with it. The problem was how to get Fiona out without disturbing the delicate balance that held everything in place.

Gibraltar walked back into the garage and stood beneath the hole. "Fiona? You need to move right to the edge. When you reach it, sit down, very carefully. Dangle your legs into the gap, and I'll do my best to help you down."

Fiona nodded, her face white and intent. She inched towards the edge, the fragile floorboards creaking beneath her weight. A shower of ash fell on Gibraltar's upturned face. He wiped it away and gestured for Fiona to come closer. Suddenly the floor cracked and she gave a shriek of terror.

"Hold on. Stay still a second – you're all right, the joist is holding. You'll be fine. Bring your legs around, very gently, and drop them through the gap."

Fiona moved so carefully, she might have been a piece of film running in slow motion. As her full weight came

58

down on the joist, the broken floorboards sagged under the load and another section fell away. A burnt plank dropped close to where Gibraltar was standing, and he dodged slightly to avoid being hit.

"Now, slide forward and drop into my arms."

"It's too far! I'll get hurt!"

"No, you won't."

"I will!" Fiona started to stand up again. As she did, the joist she was sitting on snapped with a loud crack and threw her forward. Fiona screamed and dropped through the gap. Her legs scissored frantically, but Gibraltar grabbed her as she fell. In another moment she was on the ground and they ran for their lives, dodging falling floorboards, as half the house seemed to come down in a heap behind them.

Fiona collapsed on the burnt grass in the garden, sobbing with fright at their near escape. Gibraltar laid a hand briefly on her shoulder.

"Are you all right?"

Fiona nodded. "You shouldn't have come after me," she said. "I was stupid to have gone in there. You could have been killed because of me."

"One day that might be necessary," said Gibraltar. He reached down his hand and helped Fiona to her feet. "But not, I think, tonight."

6
PLOTS AND PLANS

Emily sat with Ron at the dining-room table, propped up on a stack of cushions and eating a hearty breakfast of scrambled eggs and bacon. The horrors of the night before had vanished. Emily's wrists and ankles were still sore from being tied up, but she had slept well and her usual cheerful spirits had returned. Even Ron seemed to have become his normal self again. He was not wearing his Operation Miniver uniform this morning, but was dressed in jeans and a cotton shirt that made him look less menacing and much more like an ordinary suburban dad.

As Ron tucked into his eggs and coffee, Emily stole a look at him across the table. She was still not quite sure what to make of his sudden change of heart, but she had heard him talking on the phone to Alex and Sandra often enough that his treachery towards her and Rose was starting to make sense. Ron had sold out to Madame purely because of Alex. If their positions had been reversed, would Emily have done the same for

Rosamund? It was an uncomfortable question, and one that Emily could not really answer. In the meantime, there was something that she had done, a mistake which Emily knew she had to put right.

"Ron," she blurted out, "I'm sorry. I didn't realize Alex needed an operation."

Ron lifted his eyebrows. Emily went on in a rush, as if she was anxious to get the explanation out quickly, before the chance was gone. "I know Rose and I should have guessed you and Sandra couldn't afford it, but we didn't. If somebody had told us, we would have done something. I'm sorry. I know it doesn't change anything, but we just never knew."

"Hmm," said Ron. Emily was not sure how he had taken her apology, but he did not say anything further and after a moment, she realized he had accepted what she had said. She smiled at him, feeling enormously relieved, and, rather to her surprise, Ron smiled back.

"Good," he said. "Let's make some plans about what happens next, shall we?"

"That's easy," said Emily, feeling as relieved as Ron by the change of subject. "We have to find Rose, of course. I know exactly where to look for her. She'll be with our friend Livia Wallace in Artemisia West."

"Ah," said Ron. "There may be a problem, if you mean that little yellow house in Daventry Street.

Madame was feeling rather vengeful. I'm afraid she has burned it down."

"*What?*" Emily's pile of cushions wobbled and she almost slipped off the chair. "Rose – is she all right?"

"I think so," said Ron. "There was no one in the house when it was set on fire. But I think finding Rose will have to wait, Emily. Our first priority must be to stop Madame and Titus. Particularly Titus. He's the one making all the plans, and he's far cleverer and more dangerous than Madame could ever be. I'm not even sure what he's been up to myself."

"You're probably right," said Emily, after a moment's reflection. "It's going to be hard, though. How do you think we should go about it?"

"I'm not sure," admitted Ron. "Titus is a monster, but he's more cunning than anyone I've ever met. Whatever we come up with, he's quite likely to have thought of it first. The only thing working in our favour at the moment is that he and Madame have fallen out. Titus is holed up at the Archives. He's trying to get into some secret room Madame's obsessed with. From what I can gather, all the records of her banishment are in there. Titus plans to use them to force her to do whatever he wants."

"Has he found them?"

"I think not," said Ron. "I do know Titus tracked down some old carpenter who worked on the building when it was constructed, and that he got something out of him before he died. On the other hand, if he had actually found those banishment papers, I'd have expected him to produce them by now. Right up until yesterday afternoon, he was still relying on threats. I think that if Titus had discovered something, Madame would know."

"I've got an idea." Emily drew a deep breath. "On her birthday, Papa King gave Rose his half of the key to the Most Secret Room. He never told her why, but Gibraltar seems to think he wants her, not Madame, to succeed him as Queen of Artemisia. If we can get into the Most Secret Room before Madame and Titus, we can find Papa King's will and force Madame out. We can produce the will in Parliament, and demand that Rose be recognized as Papa King's heir."

"You're forgetting two things," Ron objected. "First, Titus is getting ready to stack the Artemisian Parliament with members of the Minivers Fan Club Committee. They're all his supporters. They're not going to let Rosamund become queen, whether she's named in Papa King's will or not."

"They're not the only MPs," insisted Emily. "And don't forget, we have Gibraltar. He's written books about the government of Artemisia. If there's a way of making Rose queen, he'll know what it is."

"All right," said Ron. "So your friend Gibraltar can

help with that. But the second problem is even harder to get around. No one, except possibly Titus, knows where the Most Secret Room is."

"You're wrong." Emily shook her head. "Someone else does know where it is. Someone who's on our side and completely trustworthy. She used to be a cleaner at the City Archives, and was the one who foiled Madame's original plot against Papa King. Our old housekeeper, Millamant."

"Millamant?" Ron was genuinely surprised. "Millamant knows where the Most Secret Room is?"

"I'm pretty sure she does," said Emily. "At any rate, she knows an awful lot about it. Madame had Milly arrested and locked up. Is she still a prisoner?"

"I believe she is," said Ron. "Titus thought she might come in useful as bait in a trap for you and Rosamund. I doubt very much anyone would have moved her in the last few days. I can probably free her quite easily, but once we do that, we'll have to act quickly. Titus keeps very close tabs on everything. We'll have a day, or two at most, before he finds out."

"Then we can't wait any longer," said Emily. "We need to get Milly out of prison, and find a way of smuggling her into the Archives."

"I suppose we might manage that," said Ron thoughtfully. "If we time our entry for tomorrow night,

Titus and Madame and most of the MFC Committee and Operation Miniver will be at Parliament House, being sworn in as MPs. The Archives should be almost empty."

Emily clapped her hands. "That's perfect!"

"We've still got to break into the building," Ron warned. "Don't forget: there are no windows. It's extremely secure."

"I've already thought of that," said Emily. "I've got a plan and I'm sure it will work. Tell me: when Madame stole all of our possessions, did she remember *Emily-Rose*?"

A gleam of understanding twinkled in Ron's eyes. He leaned back in his chair and folded his arms admiringly across his chest.

"No, she didn't," he said. "Emily, I salute you. Maybe Titus isn't going to get everything his own way, after all."

Glenda Milton, the former City Archivist, had always prided herself on keeping up appearances. In her opinion, the Archivist was a person of great importance, and she had made sure that her office was big enough and posh enough to prove it. If Glenda had been around to see what Titus had done to it since he had thrown her out, she would have been horrified. The Archivist's office looked like a demolition site, with plaster ripped from the walls, the white carpet torn away, and all the furniture Glenda had carefully chosen tossed out into the corridor like rubbish.

Holly, in charge of the work, stood watching an electrician removing light fittings from the ceiling. The air was thick with dust and several of the men were coughing, but Holly had no intention of giving them a break. She herself was dressed in overalls, with heavy boots and a hard hat on her dark, wavy hair. Holly had been working as hard as anybody, without any sign of flagging, and though several of the men were starting to look mutinous, having worked an all-night shift, they were clearly too frightened of her to protest.

"Can you see anything?" Holly asked. The electrician on the ladder shook his head and she gestured him down impatiently and climbed up the ladder herself. A hole had been punched through the ceiling plaster, and she shone a torch into the gap. Holly was still peering into the hole when the door opened and Titus came into the office with Tom McMahon.

"Any luck?" asked Titus.

"Not yet," admitted Holly. She climbed down from the ladder and gestured to the walls, where the workmen were ripping off the sheeting. "There are still some sections of plaster to come down, but there are rooms on the other side, and I doubt we'll find anything. We've searched all the most obvious places pretty carefully."

"Let's have another look at the floor plan." Titus went across to Glenda Milton's over-sized desk, which was the only item of furniture still in the room. Sheafs of rolled-up plans, some of them very old, were jumbled on its surface. Titus reached unerringly for the correct one and spread it out, pinning down one corner with a coffee cup and letting Holly hold down the other edge. He dusted off some plaster and scrutinized it carefully.

"This is the room we are in, here." He pointed to a drawing on the top of the sheet. "And this is the level below. If there is a hidden room under the floor, it obviously won't be marked on the plan, but we should still be able to work out where it is by comparing the drawings and the actual measurements of the rooms below us."

"If the Most Secret Room's there, the plan and the room won't match," said Tom McMahon, trying to sound clever. Holly shot him an impatient look.

"Yes. I've already thought of that," she said. "But the rooms beneath this office *do* match the drawings, Titus. I've measured them myself and there's no mistake. Even if we take up the whole floor and demolish the walls, I don't think we're going to find anything."

Titus furrowed his brow. "What about the ceiling?"

Holly shook her head. "There's a bit of roof space for the wiring: I was looking into it when you arrived. But I don't think there's anything there either."

"Perhaps it's all a mistake," put in Tom McMahon. "Maybe that old man was wrong, and the Most Secret Room's not here at all."

Holly looked at him with dislike. "Perhaps you could take off your fancy coat and help us prove that."

"Enough," said Titus. He moved the coffee cup off the corner of the plan and the sheet rolled up with a snap. "Holly, take down the rest of the ceiling plaster and lift the floorboards. We need to be sure we haven't missed anything. Tom, I've a theory about the basements I want to test. I need you to come with me."

Tom followed Titus reluctantly out of the office. He was feeling very tired, and wished he could go home, but he was too afraid of Titus to ask if he could leave. Still, at least he had got away from Holly. They went together down the main stairs to the deserted reading room, and from there, through a pair of swing doors into the archivists' workroom. Titus led Tom past the abandoned desks and the porters' trolleys parked beside the document lift, and pushed open a second door marked *BASEMENTS*.

"This way," he said.

The door closed behind them with a soft clunk. All

the noise filtering down from the workmen was abruptly cut off, and there was a drop in temperature that made Tom shiver. His immediate reaction was to want to run back into the lighted workroom. But Titus had already sloped away, down the dimly lit stairs to the first basement below, and Tom knew he had no real choice but to follow. At the bottom of the stairs was a huge space, filled with dusty shelves that receded into the shadows as far as Tom could see. Titus gestured towards them.

"The first level. Births. This is where everything starts, Tom. You're in there somewhere, along with everybody else who's ever been born in Artemisia. But we're not stopping here. There's a lot more interesting stuff further down."

Titus steered Tom towards another, even colder and darker staircase. The second basement was much like the first, but somehow creepier, and the third level was worse again. It was like going down, step by step, into a kind of dusty underworld made of concrete and metal girders, a world that was stuffed with secrets nobody in their right mind wanted to know. As Glenda Milton's assistant, Tom had been concerned with policy, and had never before been further than the first basement. That people actually worked on these levels was almost unbelievable, yet as they descended through the levels they passed dingy offices with single light bulbs, and desks in little clusters stacked with papers, exactly as their owners had left them. By the fourth level, the records were becoming so old, filthy and neglected it was hard to believe they would be useful for anything. Titus produced a torch and turned it on. He whispered to Tom as they passed the shelves.

"Land Records . . . Probate . . . Parliamentary Papers. . ."

Tom swallowed. Even the desks were starting to disappear, and the lighting, which had been poor, was almost nonexistent. On the staircase down to the sixth level, he stopped, unable to continue. But Titus's hand was in the small of his back, prodding him onwards, whispering in his ear.

"Just think, Tom, everything you've ever done is in here. Little pieces of paper, decaying on the shelves. They're there for ever, until you die and beyond. When you were naughty at school and the headmaster punished you. When you left your car in the disabled parking space and were fined. All your addresses, all the places that you've lived. The letter you wrote to the interview panel when you were trying to get the job. The time sheets you falsely filled in when Glenda was away."

"I can't see," said Tom in a wavering voice. He sounded like a little boy, afraid of the dark. "This theory – the one you want to test. What is it?"

"In a moment," said Titus. "We're almost there."

They were on the steps to the eighth basement. Tom stumbled down the last few broken-down treads, and found himself in what seemed to be a short, L-shaped corridor. The shadows were so thick that the feeble beam of Titus's torch was almost swallowed up. A cold sweat broke out on Tom's forehead and under his armpits. His hands felt like ice, and he could barely put one foot in front of the other. At the end of the corridor, a large 9 was painted rather crookedly on the wall. The paint had run on the bottom stroke and an arrow pointed down at a hole in the floor.

Titus knelt beside the hole. The lack of light did not seem to bother him, and Tom saw him breathing in the scent of whatever lay down below. With a chill, Tom realized that Titus was not afraid. It was almost as if he was in his native environment. If Tom could have turned at that moment and run away, he would have.

"The ninth basement," said Titus. "I think old Queen Rosamund had a sense of humour, don't you?" He took something out of his pocket. "You wanted to know what theory I wanted to test. It was to do with what the bottom basement might be useful for. Go on. Take it. You'll know what it is when you look at it."

He held out a small flat object. Reluctantly, Tom

stepped close to the edge where Titus was standing and took it. He had just enough time to recognize the security photo that he had used to denounce Titus to Madame when Titus switched off the torch.

And pushed.

The outdoor table was set for breakfast and Lindsey and Livia, Gibraltar, Rosamund and Fiona were seated under the pergola. A few bunches of grapes hung down from the vines above their head, and across the garden they could see Aunt Edie's chickens pecking contentedly at the grass. From time to time they heard the sizzle of batter from the kitchen behind them, as it hit the melted butter in the pan. Seated on three cushions to bring her up to the proper height, Rosamund helped herself to pancake number four and smothered it with extra golden syrup. It was strangely liberating to realize that even if she put on a whole extra kilo – which on a person her size would certainly show – it didn't matter a bit.

"These are delicious," said Fiona, digging into her pancake with a fork. "Do you know, I haven't eaten since Saturday night?"

"I've always said that pancakes were one of Aunt

Edie's specialities," said Lindsey, whose figure would certainly not have shown an extra kilo, or even three. "Eat up, Fiona. You're a growing girl." She offered the plate to Gibraltar, who was drinking coffee at the end of the table, apparently lost in thought. "Would you like some more?"

Gibraltar shook his head. "I've had enough, thanks. I'm just wondering about our next step. There are a couple of different ways we could go."

"Oh, Rosamund and I have already talked about that," said Lindsey. "Rose must be made queen, of course." She spoke in her usual upfront, breezy tone, but something about her words and manner made the entire table go instantly silent.

Gibraltar looked at Rosamund. "Rose?"

"Well, I don't really like the idea," Rosamund admitted. "I've never wanted to be queen for a moment. But with Emmie missing, and Madame trying to take over, what's the alternative? I'm not leaving Artemisia without Emily and Millamant. And Papa King does want me to succeed him. We know that's why he gave me the key."

"No, we don't," said Livia at once. "Not for certain; not without seeing his will. Anyway, you don't even have Papa King's key any more. Titus has it, and even he can't do anything without the other half."

"Oh, really," said Rosamund scornfully. "I suppose you

wouldn't know anything about that, would you, Livia?"

"No. I don't," Livia snapped. "And if I did, I wouldn't tell you. What about you, Rose? Is there anything you need to own up to?" There was an awkward moment. That Rosamund was apparently aware Livia had her grandfather's key was something of a shock, but Livia could not accuse her of snooping without explaining why she had kept it secret from the others. Nor could Rosamund explain how she knew Livia had it. To do that, she would have to admit that she had been searching someone else's private things.

"The keys are not particularly relevant," said Gibraltar in a firm voice. "We don't know where the Most Secret Room is, and we cannot get into it without both halves. But if I may offer an opinion, I think Livia is actually right. Rosamund can only become queen if she is named in Papa King's will, or if she is elected to that position by the Parliament of Artemisia. The problem is, Titus knows that too, and he is already working to make sure that does not happen. There is something I haven't yet told you. When I went looking for Emily, I spoke to someone I know in the palace, a woman who works closely with Madame. You might remember her too, Rosamund. Her name is Adelaide Clark."

"Adelaide!" exclaimed Rosamund. "Of course I know Adelaide. She used to be Papa King's secretary. Emily and

I had lots to do with her."

"Adelaide worked for Papa King for many years," said Gibraltar. "She knows a great deal about the background to this situation, and she is very unhappy about what's happening. According to Adelaide, there has been some sort of falling-out between Madame and Titus. Ron Burton has been more or less sacked from Operation Miniver, and the rumour is that Titus has discovered the location of the Most Secret Room."

Lindsey gave a low whistle. Rosamund sat up, taut and straight on her pile of cushions.

"But that's where Papa King's will is kept!"

"We don't know for certain that Titus has found the will," warned Gibraltar. "But yes, it does sound serious. What Titus wants is to control Madame, and rule Artemisia through her. I have little time for Papa King. I think he is largely responsible for all our problems, but at least he had his own rules and could be relied upon to stick by them. Titus has no rules at all. If we don't do something now, I believe that Artemisia is going to find itself in a far worse position than any of us could ever have imagined. I am probably the only person who has a chance of stopping Titus. To do that, I will need to speak with him alone."

Rosamund looked at Gibraltar oddly. "You talk as if you know him."

Gibraltar shook his head. "I don't think anybody truly

knows Titus. Let us say, I had a little to do with his family, a long time ago."

"But who is he?" insisted Rosamund.

"I wouldn't ask that question yet, if I were you, Rose," said Gibraltar. "There are other things that come along with the answer, and you may not like them."

"Oh, please." Livia, who since the mention of the key had been very quiet, suddenly spoke up. "Stop this. Stop it at once." She turned to Gibraltar. "You can't be serious. You want to risk your life – all our lives – to put *her* on the throne of Artemisia?"

"Have you a better suggestion?" said Gibraltar.

Livia looked around the table. Everyone's eyes were on her, even Aunt Edie's, from where she stood in the kitchen doorway with a plate of toast. All at once Livia felt angry with Rosamund, who had caused her problems, and with Lindsey and Fiona for backing her up. But most of all, Livia felt angry with Gibraltar. She knew that he had given her no encouragement; that she could not blame him for the way she felt about him. Nor, for all his willingness to help her, could she accuse him of showing any particular favouritism towards Rosamund. But the thought that he was prepared to risk his life to see this ridiculous mission through and put a two-foot-tall ex-celebrity on the throne of Artemisia was more than Livia could stand.

She stood up. "I don't care what you want to do, but

I've had enough of these crazy plans. If you think I'm going to help you go into the Archives and confront Titus, you can forget it right now."

"Nobody asked you to come," said Rosamund. "We don't need you to drive us this time. Lindsey will do it. You can stay here with Fiona, in case we hear from Emily."

"Oh, for goodness' sake," said Livia. "How on earth would Emily find us here? The chances of any of us ever seeing her again are next to nil. She's probably dead."

"I don't believe you!" Rosamund gripped the edge of the table. "Emily's alive, and whatever it takes, I am going to find her. And when I am queen, I won't forget what you just said, Livia Wallace!"

"That's assuming you become queen. Who's stupid enough to want that?"

"Plenty of people!"

"Plenty of fools. Look at you. You're only fourteen years old. You've no education, you're not even very bright. I won't stoop to point out that your size is not exactly an advantage. Oh yes, you can sing and dance. But in case you've forgotten, *Queen* Rosamund, the Minivers aren't very popular at the moment. You can blame Madame or whoever you like, but the reality is, Artemisia is *over* you."

"Livia," said Gibraltar.

Livia rounded on him. "And *you* are the biggest fool of all," she flashed, then ran sobbing into the house.

7

OPERATION MILLAMANT

Fourteen years before, when Rosamund Miniver was discovered on the hospital steps in a shoebox, she had immediately become the most famous baby in Artemisia. The papers wrote that she had been born smiling at a camera, and for once what they said was actually true. Rosamund was so pretty and had so much personality that even if she had not been so tiny, she would have attracted attention. But all babies, including famous ones, need someone to care for them. Papa King had become her foster-father, but everyone had agreed the most important man in Artemisia could hardly look after a baby by himself. It was thus decided, and announced in Parliament, that the miniature baby would have a miniature nanny. The person Papa King chose for this important task was Millamant.

At first sight, Millamant did not have a great deal to recommend her. She was certainly very small, but unlike Rosamund and Emily, she was neither dainty nor pretty and dark-haired, but thickset, blonde and extremely plain. What was not known was that Millamant was also brave and resourceful, and that Papa King owed her a great debt. When Madame and her mother Susan had attempted to murder him and seize his throne, it had been Millamant who had saved his life. Her appointment as Rosamund's nurse had been Papa King's way of saying "thank you", but the reward had given Milly far more than she had ever dreamed possible. From the moment she had laid eyes on Rosamund, and later Emily, Milly had fallen in love with them, and she adored the Minivers with a passion so fierce that no one could have doubted she would have died for them.

In recent years, as the girls had grown up and become celebrities, Millamant had become more of a housekeeper than a nurse, but she was still a very important little person. Luckily, Madame had never discovered that it was Milly who had betrayed her plot to Papa King, but she knew how protective and careful Millamant was of her charges, and for this reason she had done her best to get Millamant out of the way. As soon as Madame launched her attack on the Minivers, she had ordered Millamant's arrest. In the weeks that followed, Milly had led a wretched existence, taken from one unpleasant prison to another, uncertain whether Rosamund and Emily were even alive. She had been ill and nearly died. But though she had been sick and mistreated, Millamant had survived the terrible things that had been done to her. Now, hidden away in the hospital of the Queen Rosamund Home for Delinquent Girls, she was finally planning to escape.

Millamant was determined to discover Emily and Rosamund. She did not know for certain where they were, but she had Livia's address and was confident that if she got out, she would be able to track them down. Unfortunately her room, while not exactly a prison, was carefully locked at night, and had a barred window which even someone as small as she was could not hope to squeeze through. It appeared hopeless, but Millamant had a trick up her sleeve her captors did not know about. Millamant had been in touch briefly with some of the other prisoners, a group of girls called the Minivers Underground. They had given her some explosives from a box that they had stolen from the railway shunting yard in town, and Milly had positioned it on the windowsill and was preparing to set it off.

Millamant connected the detonator wire to the terminals, climbed down off her chair, and unwound it back to the bed. It seemed a strange thing for her to be doing, for she had always been a peaceable person who liked nothing better than to spend her evenings in front of the television with a mug of cocoa. But these days, nothing was normal. The thought that Emily and Rosamund needed her gave purpose to Millamant's actions, and she crawled under the bed, drew a deep breath, and pressed the detonator button.

The explosion deafened her. The floor shook like a wave, and she was actually picked up and dropped by the force of the blast. Millamant had not expected it to be so severe, and for several seconds everything was in such confusion she did not know what to do. The air was thick with dust, the furniture had been thrown about, and only the heavy hospital bed had stayed more or less where it was. Millamant coughed and flapped a hand in front of her face. Then she glimpsed light and realized it was coming from outside. Not only the bars, but the window and a large chunk of wall had disappeared in a shower of masonry and glass.

Millamant ran to what was left of the window and heaved herself on to the broken wall. She did not find this easy, for she was not nearly as fit as Rosamund or Emily, and though the drop to the ground was not far, it was so scary to someone of her tiny size that she almost gave up on the spot. Then an alarm went off, shrill and terrifyingly close, and she jumped and fell, knocking all the breath from her lungs. A sharp pain shot through Millamant's knee and she felt the skin rip from her hands. She tried to get up, but she was not young, and had been very sick, and by the time she managed to limp away from the window, the alarm had been joined by the sound of shouting voices in the distance.

Soon the grounds would be swarming with people, all looking for her. She had to get out of sight as quickly as possible, or everything she had done would be in vain. Millamant hobbled as fast as she could towards some bushes, but she knew that these would be the first place the search parties would look. There was an access road ahead, but it led only to a security gate, and at the other end, a car park. For a wild moment Millamant wondered if she could steal one of the cars that were dotted around it. It was a stupid thought, for she could barely drive Rosamund and Emily's miniaturized bubble cars, let alone one with normal-sized controls, but she was now so desperate that she would have tried anything. Millamant made up her mind. She veered away from the bushes and ran for the car park gate. She had almost reached it when suddenly a spotlight lit up the asphalt ahead of her. It danced towards her, another joined it, and right at the moment their beams crossed, she was caught and held in their relentless glare.

Milly ran on, but the beams had locked on her position and she could not shrug them off. A car sounded behind her, driving very fast, and as she reached the carpark, it swung around her and screeched to a halt. It was a white van, horrifyingly familiar to her, and as Milly tried vainly to dive under one of the nearest cars, its driver's door flung open and a hand reached down and grabbed her. Milly fought and kicked, but she was still weak from being ill, and could not resist very hard. A moment later, she was hauled up like a dog from beneath a sofa.

"I thought you were supposed to be looking after her," said a man's voice, panting slightly. "If I'd arrived five minutes later, she would have been gone."

A second pair of footsteps came hurrying across the asphalt. It was the Governor of the Queen Rosamund Home, generally known to the girls as Sharkface. She produced a pair of handcuffs and snapped them on Millamant's wrists, ratcheting them down to fit. Milly almost snarled at her, like the little bulldog she resembled.

"You'll have to sign her out," said Sharkface in a disapproving voice.

"Was she ever signed in?" asked Ron. Millamant could not see his face, but she had known at once it was him. Her heart pounded with a sick kind of fear. Ron had joined forces with Madame against Rosamund and Emily, whom he was sworn to protect. He had locked

Millamant in prison and let Madame misuse her so badly that she had nearly died. This last sin, Millamant could forget, but not the first. She believed firmly in loving her own enemies, but it was much harder to forgive someone who had treated her beloved Rosamund and Emily so treacherously.

Sharkface shook her head. Millamant had always been a secret prisoner. There was no record that she had ever been in the Queen Rosamund Home, and Sharkface clearly knew it. She handed Ron the key to the handcuffs and he opened the back of the van. Milly struggled again, but she knew her escape had failed. She was thrust into the van, and a moment later it started up and drove off down the access road towards the gate.

Milly lay on the floor, surrounded by ropes and piles of blankets. The fight had gone out of her and she felt old and tired and ill. It was over. She had lost her bid for freedom, and she would never see Emily and Rosamund again. A tear trickled down her dirty cheek, and as Ron drove through the security gate and out on to the road back to the centre of town, she began to sob. In the darkness beside her, she sensed something moving under one of the blankets. A small hand caught hers, and the blanket was thrown back and a familiar face looked out.

"Milly. It's all right. Please don't cry."

"Emily!" The shock was so great that for a moment, Millamant's heart actually stopped. "Oh my darling, have they got you too?"

"Don't worry, Milly. It's all right. You're being rescued." Emily stood on tiptoe and reached over to the front seat. To Millamant's utter amazement, Ron tossed her the key to the handcuffs and smiled.

"I don't understand," Millamant began. The key clicked in the lock and the handcuffs clattered on to the floor. Millamant stared at them, then threw herself with a cry into Emily's arms.

For the first time in weeks, it seemed as if the world had gone right side up.

In her rooms in the royal palace, Madame was playing with her cat, Kitty. For many years while she had lived in lonely exile with her mad mother, Susan, Kitty had been Madame's only companion. They had endured rejection and poverty together; and Kitty had shared all Madame's secrets. It was true to say that Madame loved Kitty with all her heart. Since her heart was a small and shrivelled one, this was not saying a great deal; nevertheless, the fact that she had given all of it had to count for something.

Kitty had never been a very playful cat, and was inclined to scratch, but Madame had recently developed a game which was a favourite with both of them. First, she would make herself a supper of sardine sandwiches, and eat them while Kitty prowled around her feet, mewing with hunger. Madame would then pour the last oil from the tin on to a piece of scrunched-up newspaper and dangle it on a string in front of Kitty's nose. Since Kitty was not very well fed, the smell of the fish on the paper normally drove her wild. She would mew and jump and they would have a fine old time as Madame snatched the paper out of Kitty's reach when she tried to catch it.

Tonight, though, Kitty seemed not to want to play, and after a few half-hearted snatches at the paper, she crawled under Madame's threadbare sofa to sulk. Madame's eyes strayed to the tin of cat food on the table. A local firm had recently offered Kitty free food for life. In exchange for this, a series of ads had appeared in magazines, in which Kitty, far fatter and glossier than she had ever appeared in real life, had endorsed the cheapest and nastiest cat food on the market as being used at the Artemisia Palace. Madame had been very pleased with the savings on cat food, but tonight she was starting to wonder if she had made a mistake. A Kitty who was too full to play was not much of a companion, and a fat Kitty would sooner or later result in expensive vet bills. Perhaps now was the time to cut back on her rations. Madame picked up the half-empty tin and looked at the little scraps of fish in jelly that nestled in the bottom. Really, the food didn't look too bad at all. She could almost eat it herself. . .

A sharp rap on the door jerked Madame out of her thoughts with an unpleasant start. She looked at the clock, saw that it was half past nine, and frowned. Who could possibly be visiting at this hour? A picture of Titus flashed into her head and her fingers clenched involuntarily around the smelly ball of newspaper. She would not see him; she would *not*. Nobody could make her let him in. Madame looked around wildly for somewhere to hide, and saw Kitty already disappearing into the adjoining bedroom. If only she had not left the light on. . .

The rap sounded again and a woman's voice called out to her from the corridor. "Madame? Madame, are you there? It's Nurse Agatha. I need to speak with you, urgently."

The name and voice sounded familiar. Madame struggled to place them, and finally remembered that Nurse Agatha was one of the nurses who cared around the clock for Papa King. Very carefully, for she was not entirely convinced it wasn't a trick, Madame unbolted and unlocked the door, keeping on the safety chain just in case. A short woman in a white nurse's uniform was standing outside in the corridor.

"Hello?" said Madame cautiously.

The nurse peered around the crack in the door. "May I come in?"

Madame reluctantly unhooked the safety chain. She opened the door just enough to let the nurse inside, then snapped it closed and shot home the bolt. Nurse Agatha took a few steps into the room, looking around her as she did. She paused by the sofa, but Madame did not ask her to sit down.

Nurse Agatha cleared her throat nervously. "I need to speak to you about your father."

"My father?" For a moment, Madame was at a loss. It was so long since she had actually thought of Papa King as a parent that she was almost surprised to realize that Nurse Agatha was talking about him. "Why? Is something the matter?"

Nurse Agatha nodded. "I'm sorry, but he's taken a turn for the worse. I thought you ought to know."

Madame stared at her in dismay. "Has he had another stroke?"

"Oh, no. Nothing like that. But his blood pressure is high, which isn't good, and there's definitely been a change in him mentally. He's very upset about something and keeps trying to talk. Of course, no one can understand what he's saying, and that just makes him more distressed."

"Sedate him," said Madame at once. She knew quite well that Papa King was upset because of what he had discovered about the Minivers. The last thing she wanted was for him to give away any details. She added unctuously, "It's the kindest thing to do."

"Yes . . . well, I can do that, of course. But there's something about his condition I don't like. It's as if – well, as if he's giving up. With your permission, I'd like to call in the doctor. I know he's not due until Friday, but—"

"Bring him in," said Madame. She winced as she said this, for the doctor's visits were extremely expensive, and she normally did everything she could to stave them off. But this was not a time to quibble about money. It was vital that Papa King should stay alive until she had dealt with Titus and secured her claim to the throne. When that had happened, she would dispose of Papa King herself. It would be lovely, absolutely wonderful, to finally conclude the job she had botched so many years before. But for the moment, until she had resolved the issue of the Most Secret Room and its contents, it was a pleasure that would have to wait.

Madame waited until Nurse Agatha had left, looking

surprised and cheerful at what she assumed was her employer's change of heart, and re-locked and re-bolted her door. The game with Kitty had lost its savour. Madame put on her nightdress, switched off the single low-wattage light bulb, and climbed into bed.

After such an interruption, it was hardly likely that she would find it easy to get to sleep. Try as she might, though she closed her eyes and counted as many sheep as she could conjure up (thin, scrawny sheep, the sort that would be made into budget lamb chops), Madame could not settle down. Her heart was racing, her stomach felt twisted and upset, and her head swam with dreadful images of Titus. What was he doing? Had he got into the Most Secret Room yet? Madame saw him, opening the door and running his fingers over the file boxes of papers. She saw him standing up on television and telling her secrets to the world. Then she saw herself trying to counter his accusations, all in white and looking tragic and bereft.

"I was very young," she said. "I didn't know what I was doing."

"Liar!" Titus shouted. "You went into your father's room while he was sleeping and tried to burn him in his bed. You should be locked up for ever!"

"It was an accident!" she pleaded. "I didn't realize what might happen. Please, believe me!" She turned to the cameras that were rolling as she spoke. Tears poured down her cheeks and she wrung her hands in front of the audience. "Please! I beg you, give me another chance!"

"Not a hope!" said Titus. He leaned forward and Madame saw that the TV studio had turned into a chamber of the Artemisia Parliament, and that Titus was sitting on the throne reserved for Papa King. The other seats were filled with members of the Minivers Fan Club Committee and as they began to boo and jeer her, Titus stood up like an executioner and advanced, dangling Papa King's key on a chain from his finger. Suddenly, Madame let out a scream and sat up, bolt upright in her bed.

The sound of her own voice woke Madame up. She struggled with her bedding, which had somehow pulled itself up over her head, and threw it off. Her dream evaporated like mist, but the image of Titus dangling the key on its chain stayed with her. He must not get hold of the key. He *must not*.

A kind of madness gripped Madame, and she jumped out of bed. Kitty was underneath it, crouched beside her threadbare slippers, and she mewed and wriggled as Madame hauled her out. The little tin was still secured to her collar. Madame wrestled with the wire that held it. As Kitty lashed out with her claws, it snapped and fell on the floor.

"Ow!" Madame snatched up the tin containing the key print. She hurried into the bathroom, dropped it into the toilet and pulled the chain, before she had a chance to regret her action. The rush of water from the cistern swirled around the bowl and down the bend, carrying with it all her hopes. She had stopped Titus, but the tin had taken with it any chance that she might get into the Most Secret Room herself. Madame staggered out of the bathroom, flung herself down on to her bed and wept.

8
EMILY-ROSE

Livia was in disgrace. Since her outburst at the breakfast table, she had locked herself in Lindsey's bedroom and refused to come out. Lindsey had tried to reason with her, but she had been ignored. Aunt Edie had taken a salad sandwich up at lunch time, yet four hours later the sandwich was still sitting on its plate outside the door. When Gibraltar had gone to speak with her, Livia had told him in a muffled voice to go away.

"I don't know why you're bothering," said Rosamund, when Gibraltar came downstairs to report his failure. "I'm sure I don't care if she's upset, after the things she said to me. I'm not going to talk to her again until she apologizes."

"Livia's normally very reasonable," said Gibraltar. "She'll calm down eventually, but right now she's just not ready to. And she is entitled to her opinion. Don't forget, Rose, that she helped you and gave you a roof over your head when nobody else wanted anything to do with the Minivers."

"I don't care. I will never forgive her for saying that Emily was dead."

"Never is a very long time."

"Then she'll have a long time to regret she ever said it," retorted Rosamund. "Oh, please, Gibraltar. Let's stop talking about Livia and decide what we're going to do. We need to be making plans, not arguing."

"I've already made my plans," said Gibraltar. "I told you I was going to speak to Titus alone. I never said I'd take you with me."

Rosamund's face creased with disappointment. "But that's not fair. Why not?"

"To be blunt, you'll be in my way," said Gibraltar. "There's nothing you can do, and it would be putting you at risk for no reason. Also, I would have to look after you, and I will be quite busy enough looking out for myself."

"But what if Emily's there?"

"Then you'll have to trust me to look after her."

"I do trust you," said Rosamund after a tiny pause. "But I still want to go. What if something happens to you? Gibraltar, what if you don't come back? I can't be queen by myself. What sort of ruler would I be if you weren't there to help me?"

"A very elegant one, with lots of shoes," said Gibraltar, with a little smile. Rosamund stamped her foot.

"Stop making jokes. You know I don't want to be queen without you to tell me what to do. It would be terrible, I'd hate it. Gibraltar, *please*. You can't leave me behind. I know it's dangerous, but I've been in danger before."

"No," said Gibraltar, suddenly serious again. "I'm sorry, Rose, but I've made up my mind. You're not coming." He took her hand in his large one. "Believe me, I know what I'm doing."

At these words, Rosamund's hope died. She knew Gibraltar well enough by now to tell when there was no point in arguing further. For a few terrible seconds Rosamund even thought she was going to cry, but the long years of having to behave perfectly in public paid off, and she forced herself to nod as if she agreed. There was only one occasion when Rosamund had failed to behave as a Miniver should, and that was at her birthday party, on the night she was kidnapped. No matter how confused and unhappy she felt, she would die sooner than let herself down like that again.

"I'll go and ask Lindsey if I can borrow her car," said Gibraltar. He stood up and Rosamund watched him head out into the garden, where Lindsey was weeding one of the flower beds. She did not know what to do, but she felt certain that if she did not go with Gibraltar, something terrible would happen either to him or to

Emily, the two people she cared most for in all the world. Despite what Livia had said, and despite her own earlier misgivings, Rosamund was now convinced that Emily was alive. It was to do with their being Minivers, and the only people of their kind. Emily had been in great danger and perhaps come close to death, but if she had actually died, Rosamund knew she would somehow have felt it. On the other hand, she did not know where Emily was, whether she was safe, and whether she was a prisoner of Madame or Titus. The fact that Adelaide had been unable to tell Gibraltar where she was made Rosamund suspect Emily must be with Titus, and that only made her feel more frightened than ever.

The feeling of unease stayed with Rosamund all through dinner. It was a meal nobody particularly wanted, and which Livia did not come down for. As soon as it was over, Rosamund went into the living room. She found Fiona curled up on the sofa with Aunt Edie's elderly dachshund, Rupert, reading a magazine. Rosamund did not like dogs much, but she clambered up on to the sofa and gave Rupert a cautious pat. She was relieved when the dog merely lifted his head and put it down again.

"Fiona, I need your help."

"*My* help?" Fiona laid her magazine aside. "What on earth for?"

"Shh!" Rosamund put her finger to her lips. "I don't want anyone to overhear us. Gibraltar's getting ready to go to the Archives and speak to Titus. He wants to go alone. I need you to help me get into the car without him knowing."

It was obvious from Fiona's expression that she was unimpressed. Rosamund stood up on the sofa cushions, so that she and Fiona were at eye level, and did her best to make her understand.

"Please, Fiona. I've got to go. It's a feeling I've got that I can't explain, but I know something awful's going to happen. All I want you to do is open the car door for me and tell the others I've gone to bed early. I'll never get into that Land Rover by myself. I can't even reach the door handle."

"Gibraltar must have a reason for not wanting you to go," said Fiona doubtfully. "Are you sure this is a good idea?"

"No," said Rosamund honestly. "I'm not sure. Part of me can't even believe I'm disobeying him. The only argument I ever had with Emily was because she didn't do what Gibraltar told her. But I have to go, Fiona. It's Emily. I'm sure she's at the Archives, and if anything happened to her and I wasn't there, I would never forgive myself."

That something might endanger Emily was the one

argument Fiona could not withstand. Her white, freckled face looked worried, and Rosamund knew that she was wavering. There had always been some fans who preferred one Miniver sister to the other, and while Fiona admired Rosamund, she loved Emily from the bottom of her heart. For a few more seconds she struggled with her conscience, then she put Rupert gently down on to the floor and stood up.

"I think the key's on a hook in the kitchen. I'll go and get it."

Fiona disappeared into the kitchen. While she was gone, Rosamund stole over to the French doors and looked out into the darkened garden. The big car was waiting in the driveway outside the front door, and she noticed that someone had put a ladder on the roof rack. Fiona came back with the keys and they crept out on to the drive, their feet making little crunching sounds on the gravel. Fiona unlocked and opened the car door and gave Rosamund a boost into the back seat. The car was so high off the ground and the door so heavy that there was no way Rosamund could have managed it herself.

"I'll have to lock you in," Fiona warned.

"That's fine," said Rosamund. "I don't think Gibraltar will be very long. I'll just sit here, in the very back. If anybody asks where I am, tell them I'm in the bath." She climbed over the seat into the luggage compartment and crouched down out of sight. Fiona locked the car and went back into the house.

Rosamund had never been a very patient person, but the stakes tonight were so high that for once she did not mind waiting. About half an hour passed before the house door opened and Gibraltar came out. He got into the car and started the engine, and the Land Rover roared off down the long drive, showering gravel under its wheels.

As they rounded the first curve, Rosamund glanced back at the house. There was a light burning in an upstairs window and for a moment she thought she saw someone standing there. Then the car disappeared around the bend, and whoever had been watching them was lost to view.

For the rest of her life, whenever she was asked about the happiest moment she had ever known, Millamant unhesitatingly said that it was when she and Emily were reunited in the back of Ron's van. The hours which followed her rescue passed in a sort of blissful blur. Even having Ron with them could not spoil the fact that she and Emily had weeks of explanations and catching up to do. Back home at Ron's, they sat drinking tea and talking until daylight, and then they went to sleep and woke and talked all over again. Emily was simply glad to have Millamant safe. But Ron was anxious about Madame and Titus, and late in the afternoon he told them he wanted to get their plans moving as quickly as possible.

"I quite agree," said Milly unexpectedly. "It's time somebody put an end to all this nonsense. Mind you, I still can't see Rose as queen. She's a good girl, but far too flighty. Besides, isn't all this a little premature? Papa King isn't dead."

"The last time I saw him, Papa King wasn't looking very well," said Ron, with a sideways glance at Emily. "I'm not a doctor, but I wouldn't depend on his being around for very much longer. It may seem callous, Millamant, but we need to be making plans before he dies. That's why we have to get into the Most Secret Room and find his will. Emily says you might know where the room is."

Millamant nodded. "Indeed, I do."

"Where is it, Milly?" asked Emily. "No one else has been able to find it, even Titus."

"In the Archivist's office, of course," said Milly. "It's the obvious place for it to be. You'd never expect Papa King to go traipsing down into those awful basements, would you?"

"I suppose not," said Emily. She was a little surprised

that no one had thought of this before. Of course, it would explain why Livia had never found it. Emily guessed she wouldn't have been allowed into that part of the building.

"If you can get me to the Archivist's Office, I can certainly show you where the Most Secret Room is," said Millamant. "But I don't see the point. Unless you have those two keys, you won't be able to get in."

"Not necessarily." Ron produced a wicked-looking jemmy. "Forced entry, Milly. Madame and Titus need to keep the fact that they've been in the room secret. I don't see why that need matter to us."

"It'll be a smash and grab," explained Emily. "We're going to travel in *Emily-Rose*. Ron says it's still on the helipad at Lakeheath. He can fly us straight to the Archives and land on the roof tonight, while Titus is at Parliament House."

"The building should be nearly empty for a couple of hours around nine o'clock," said Ron. "It's the best chance we're likely to get."

"And after that?" said Millamant.

"We find the papers in the Most Secret Room before Titus does," said Emily. "We use them to stop Madame. Then we make Rosamund queen."

"We'll have to find her, first," said Ron. "Let's concentrate on the first part of the plan, shall we? I'll make us something to eat, and then we should think about heading off. It's going to be a long night."

They left under cover of darkness at around seven o'clock. Ron had put on his Minivers Security uniform again, and they travelled in the white van, which Ron said had the advantage of being known to belong to Operation Miniver. So far, nobody in the task force knew that he had changed sides. He had been carrying on throughout the day as if everything was completely normal, telephoning Primrose, and giving orders for the team to investigate "sightings" of the Minivers on the other side of the city. Just before they left, Primrose phoned and told him that she and most of the security force were heading for Parliament House.

"That should keep them nicely out of our hair," said Ron in a satisfied voice, as they backed out of the driveway and headed towards the city. "Lakeheath is a private aerodrome, so I doubt there'll be anyone there to see us. It should be pretty much deserted at this time of night."

"Good," said Millamant. "I'm starting to think I'm a little too old for all this adventure stuff."

There were roadblocks on the streets around Parliament House as they passed through the city, but the traffic was flowing smoothly, and they soon reached the south-western suburbs. Lakeheath Aerodrome was where rich people and big companies kept their private planes and helicopters. It had a small control tower, a reception and lounge for travellers, and a range of hangars and outbuildings. There was a checkpoint at the main gate, but Ron showed the security guard his Operation Miniver ID card, and they were waved through without a second glance.

"So far, so good," said Ron, as they drove through the gate and down the access road. The aerodrome was well lit and dotted with light planes. One was coming in to land as they approached the helipads at the far end of the tarmac. "Look. We were right. *Emily-Rose* is still there."

Emily stood up in the back of the van and craned to see. *Emily-Rose* was the Minivers' private helicopter. In the days of their fame and glory, she and Rosamund had used it to get quickly to their public appearances, when the crowds would have made it dangerous to travel any other way. They had even employed their own helicopter pilot, a woman called Tess who would land *Emily-Rose* on the Miniver House lawn whenever they wanted to go somewhere. Emily wondered briefly what had happened to Tess. Like all the other people who had worked for her and Rosamund, she supposed she was out of a job.

Luckily, Ron also had a helicopter pilot's licence, and

had flown *Emily-Rose* on a number of occasions. The helicopter was painted pale blue and silver, with a sweeping red Minivers letter $\mathcal{M}$ emblazoned on the tail. For the first time, it struck Emily that it was a rather conspicuous aircraft, and she wondered nervously what people would think when they saw it hovering over the city. But there was nothing they could do about that. Ron stopped the car at the side of the helipad and leaned over his seat to speak to her and Millamant.

"This is as close as I can get without attracting attention," he said. "It's a pity everything here is so brightly lit, because you don't know who's watching. I know Titus has been after me ever since I hit him and we could have been followed. I'll open up the chopper and start the engine. When I give the word, run quickly across and jump in."

Ron got out of the cab and opened the back to get the jemmy, which he had stowed in an old fertilizer sack. Emily and Millamant waited inside the back of the van, watching as Ron ran across to the helicopter and unlocked the door. They briefly lost sight of him; then there was a low judder and a burst of fumes from the exhaust outlet, followed by a high-pitched whine as the engine began to build. The rotors started to spin in long, slow revolutions. Emily saw Ron gesturing wildly from the cockpit. Emily glanced around, and noticed a security camera pointed in their direction, and for the first time she heard the sound of a car's squealing brakes.

She shoved Millamant out on to the tarmac and they ran as fast as they could towards the open cabin door.

"I can't get in!" cried Milly ahead of her, and Emily saw that Ron had forgotten to put down the special step that she and Rosamund used to get into the machine. The noise of the engine was now deafening and she could tell that Ron was intent on the controls and could not hear or see what was happening. Emily yelled again, and perhaps because he heard, perhaps because he was checking whether they were safely in the cabin, Ron glanced over his shoulder.

A small vehicle was racing towards them across the tarmac. It looked like one of the little white utility vehicles that zipped around the aerodrome, and there were four people in it, dressed in the pale-blue shirts of Operation Miniver. At the sight of them, Emily uttered a loud shriek.

"They've found us!" she shouted. "Ron! Ron, we can't get in!"

Emily jumped up and down on the tarmac and Ron realized what the problem was. He wrenched off his headset and vaulted out of his seat into the passenger side. Millamant reached up her arms and he seized her wrists and yanked her bodily into the machine. Emily had grabbed hold of the edge and swung herself off her feet. She was very strong, considering her size, but it was still too far for her to pull herself up into the cabin. A strong hand took hold of her clothes and she was flipped up roughly on to the cabin floor.

Ron slammed the door closed, jumped back into the cockpit and pulled out the throttle. The engine noise was still building, its whine now drowned by the familiar chopping sound of the rotors. There was a burst of furious talk from Rob's discarded headset. Ron ripped out the wire and jammed it back on his head

"That was the control tower," he shouted. "Excuse me for not paying any attention to them. Hold on, ladies. We're in for a rough ride." He grasped the cyclic stick and pushed down his foot, and *Emily-Rose* lifted shakily into the air and sped away.

The members of the Minivers Fan Club Committee were sitting in the City Archivist's office, surrounded by dust and dirt. The search for the Most Secret Room had finished for the day, and the weary workmen had all gone home. The committee members were waiting for the cars that would take them to Parliament House, where they were about to be made MPs. Only Titus walked up and down the room, his eyes flicking around impatiently, as if searching for something the workmen had missed.

He looked completely different to his usual scruffy self. The black jeans and Minivers T-shirt were gone, replaced by a beautifully cut grey suit, a silk tie, and a crisply ironed shirt with gold cufflinks. Titus's unruly hair had been slicked back behind his ears, and if it had not been for his cold grey eyes, which nothing could alter, even people who knew him well might not have recognized him. When he came to a halt in front of the little group, the committee members sat up straight, like schoolchildren with a strict teacher. Ron was not there, of course, but Holly had changed out of her overalls into high heels and a clingy red dress, and even Brenda had put on her best clothes. She had gained weight since she had last worn them, and they did not fit very well, but Titus was not so much concerned with how she looked as to how she and the others behaved.

"Some last-minute instructions about Phase Three of our plan," he said. "I have told Madame that she must have the four of us sworn in as MPs, or certain documents will be made public. Of course, other things will happen tonight that she is not expecting. You will say nothing, and do nothing unless instructed by me. Do you understand?"

The prospective MPs nodded. Holly looked rather

excited; Brenda, merely scared. Len, who worked at the palace and had more to do with Madame than any of the others, frowned and put up his hand to ask a question.

"What if Madame asks to see the documents?"

Titus shook his head. "She won't ask. She's too frightened of what might be in them to risk their being shown in Parliament."

"It's a risk for you, too," Len insisted. "You haven't found them, yet. Sooner or later you'll have to produce them, and if you can't, Madame won't keep doing what you tell her. I know her. She's a coward, but she's not stupid."

"I'm quite aware of what I am doing," said Titus, coldly. "Keep your mouth shut, all of you, and there will be no difficulty. Just remember, it's in your interest to do as I say."

There was a tap on the door and Primrose looked into the room. "Your cars have arrived, sir."

"Good." Titus picked up a leather briefcase and gestured to the others to leave. As the group passed down the polished mahogany staircase and into the glittering entrance hall at the front of the building, Titus spoke in an undertone to Primrose.

"Ron?"

Primrose nodded. "I sent a team to intercept him an hour ago."

"Good." Titus nodded. "Consider yourself the new Chief of Operation Miniver." They reached the huge double-fronted doors and Primrose opened them to let everybody out. Two limousines were pulled up, waiting in the street. Titus walked out of the building and stood for a moment at the top of the steps. Then he locked the bronze doors shut behind him and the limousines drove away.

9
THE PURSUIT

As soon as the helicopter left the ground, Emily knew that they were in serious trouble. It was bad enough to have been followed by Operation Miniver, but now they had the control tower to worry about as well. A siren went off, so loud it could be heard even above the surge of the helicopter's rotors, and a powerful wash of light filled the sky around them. The glare followed the chopper as it rose above the helipad and flew away at a steep angle, so dazzling that Emily winced and screwed up her eyes.

"Searchlights," shouted Ron, from the cockpit. "Hold on. I've got to try and shake them off."

The helicopter banked sharply and Emily and Millamant were thrown across the carpeted floor of the cabin. Neither of them had managed to strap themselves into their seats before they had taken off, and as Ron did his best to evade the lights, throwing the controls first this way and then that, the two of them rolled across the floor like pebbles in the bottom of a barrel. Emily cannoned into the front row of seats, grabbed a metal support, and clung on for dear life.

"Get ready!" shouted Ron from the front. "Banking port . . . now!"

Emily had forgotten which side was port and which was starboard, but both she and Millamant dropped flat against the carpet. The floor tipped sharply to the left and the two passengers were flung sideways. Emily's arm was yanked almost out of its socket, but she just managed to keep hanging on to the seat. The helicopter briefly straightened, jigged up and down, and went lurching in the opposite direction. Emily wished she had not eaten before leaving the house. If the shaking went on for much longer, she was sure she was going to be sick.

The helicopter continued its erratic climb. After a while the lurching seemed to stop and they levelled out. Emily opened her eyes and saw that they had outflown the searchlights.

Emily scrambled to her feet. Through the window she could see the bright glow of the aerodrome fading rapidly, and for a moment, she thought everything was all right. Then something so loud and fast Emily barely recognized it flashed past them, whisker-close. Emily recoiled and screamed.

"A plane! Ron! We're being followed!"

Ron hauled at the controls. The helicopter dropped suddenly, making Milly and Emily fly up and go bouncing down with a thump that made them scream all over again. The plane had buzzed right in front of the cockpit, and was looping back for another pass.

"They're trying to force us to land," Ron shouted. "Hang on, ladies." He pushed the cyclic stick forward and the helicopter swooped down. For a few seconds, Emily wondered if Ron was going to land, and then she realized that he was trying to shake off their pursuers by flying as close to the ground as possible. Through the cabin window she saw the lights in the houses below them getting nearer and nearer, until they were flying so low that she could almost see the people in their living rooms, and the branches of the trees in the gardens whipping back and forth in the wash from their rotor.

The plane was now close behind them again. It was much faster than the helicopter, but less manoeuvrable. Ron flew across a highway, keeping just ahead of it. A huge set of high-voltage powerlines appeared in front of them, horribly close.

"Ron!" Emily shouted. "Don't! *Don't!*" Her tiny voice was lost in the roar of the helicopter's engines. She closed her eyes. The chopper dived and passed underneath the wires. The plane shot over the top and disappeared into the distance and a moment later, *Emily-Rose* was alone in the sky.

Emily stood up on wobbly legs and climbed on to her special Minivers-sized seat. Ron glanced over his shoulder.

"Are you all right, Emily?"

"Just bumped and bruised." As Emily replied, Millamant shakily picked herself up off the carpet and sat down beside her. "Milly's all right, too."

"Sorry about that," said Ron. "I'm afraid this hasn't worked out as well as I hoped. I think the plane's given up for the moment, but they'll be following us on radar from the aerodrome. What do you want to do now? If you like, we can forget all this and I can fly you out of Artemisia."

Emily shook her head. "They'll follow us wherever we go. Rose and I promised we'd never leave each other. We might as well finish what we started."

Ron nodded. "Strap yourselves in, then. Let's make this trip as quick as we possibly can."

He pointed the helicopter's nose towards the city and opened up the throttle.

The Land Rover nosed its way down the narrow lane beside the City Archives. It was dark, and the blank wall above the car seemed to lean on an angle, as if the whole structure was going to fall down. At the end of the lane, close to the river, was a tiny car park with three parking spaces, reserved for the use of senior staff. Gibraltar pulled into the one labelled *ASSISTANT CITY ARCHIVIST* and turned off the engine.

"You can come out now, Rose," he called. "You don't have to keep hiding. I know you're there."

There was a moment's delay. Something rustled in the darkness and then Rosamund's head popped up over the back seat.

"How could you tell?" she demanded. "Did I make a noise?"

"No," said Gibraltar. "But I suspected something was up. Whatever excuses you asked Fiona to make for you, you're just not the sort of girl who goes to bed at seven o'clock at night." He added, "Or the sort who gets up at seven in the morning, either."

Rosamund shook her head "You're quite wrong, there," she said. "When Emily and I were filming *The Minivers' Music Hour*, we had to be at the studio for our make-up every day at half past six."

"I stand corrected." When she had first met Gibraltar, Rosamund had found this sort of half-serious, half-joking manner outrageous. Now, the fact that she had once had a career as Artemisia's most famous celebrity seemed unbelievably ridiculous even to herself. She smiled, but Gibraltar's teasing expression had disappeared, and she could tell that he was completely serious. "The fact remains, Rose, you're here, when I specifically told you to stay behind. I'd like to think you can give me a good reason why you found it so necessary to disobey my instructions."

"Well. . ." Rosamund twined her hands uncomfortably around the headrest supports. "I suppose I didn't want you to go alone. I wanted to help you."

"I've already told you that you can't do that. Didn't you believe me?" Gibraltar waited, and when her reply did not come, he went on, "What has to be said is between Titus and me. He will not thank me for speaking out, and if you, of all people, are there, it could ruin everything. I've a good mind to order you to stay in the car."

I'm afraid Titus will kill you. The words trembled on Rosamund's lips, but she did not utter them. She felt very small and very stupid. Of course, she had done the wrong thing. She had known this, even when she was climbing into the car. But somehow, Rosamund had persuaded herself that once she was there, Gibraltar would be pleased to have her help. At any rate, she had thought, it could not be worse than sitting at home again, waiting anxiously for him to return.

Now, seeing Gibraltar's disapproval, she realized that it was worse, and that there was nothing in the world more wretchedly useless than being a Miniver. If only she had been a normal size she could have come and gone without people recognizing who she was, or putting herself and everyone around her into danger. A fleeting image entered her head of what life might be like as an ordinary teenager; a pretty girl with an unremarkable singing voice who lived a routine, unexceptional life. For months now, Rose had dreamed of that unattainable miracle, but never more so than since she had met Gibraltar. If Livia had wanted to come, would he have let her? The thought that the answer might be yes was like a physical pain, so secret she could not even admit it to herself.

"Well, Rosamund?" said Gibraltar, gently. "What do you intend to do?"

"I don't know," Rosamund whispered. The tears were very close, but she just managed to hold them back. "I'm . . . sorry."

Gibraltar got out of the car and came around to the back where Rosamund was standing. He opened the hatch and helped her down.

Rosamund looked at him disbelievingly. "You're letting me come?"

"If I'd realized earlier, I would have taken you back," Gibraltar said. "But it's too late now, and I suspect it would be more dangerous for you to stay in the car. If a security guard found it, you'd be trapped. But you need to know, Rose, I'm very unhappy about this. Your being here complicates things quite badly. I want you to promise that you'll do exactly as I tell you, particularly when we see Titus. No matter what happens then, you must keep your mouth shut."

Rosamund nodded. "I promise."

"I'll be holding you to that," said Gibraltar. "We're not playing games, tonight. We have to be ready for anything."

Gibraltar lifted the ladder down from the roof rack and led Rosamund across the car park. He seemed to know exactly where he was going, which surprised her a little, until she remembered that he had worked here for a time as a porter. There were no doors or windows, but a metal fire escape hung off the wall of the building, and Gibraltar's ladder was just long enough to reach it. Though Rosamund's dancing career had made her extremely fit, her short legs had to work extra hard to climb it, and they began to fail her long before they reached the top. On the last landing, she sat down briefly to catch her breath.

"How are we going to get inside?" she asked.

"There's a door on the roof," said Gibraltar. "It's the only one I know of in the entire building, apart from the big bronze ones at the front. It was old Queen Rosamund who had the Archives built. She was paranoid about security: that's why there are hardly any doors or windows. When I worked here, I used to wonder what would happen if the place ever caught fire. Hundreds of people, trapped in those evil basements. But the old queen would never have thought of that."

Rosamund had been inside the basements when she had first gone into hiding. It was unpleasant to think that Papa King had chosen to name her after someone who had cared so little about other people.

"If I become queen, I will be different," she said seriously.

"I'm sure you will," said Gibraltar. "Come on. Only one more flight to go."

They laboured up the final steps on to the roof. It was flat, with a low parapet to stop people falling off, and in the centre was a large glass pyramid, which looked like some kind of skylight. Rosamund tried to peer through the smoky glass panels, but Gibraltar told her that it was not the way into the building, and that the door was over to the side.

"The skylight's over the Archivist's office," he explained. "I believe Glenda Milton put it in because she thought it was too dark in there. Pity she didn't think about the rest of us." He took off his backpack, produced a hammer and a sharp chisel, and set to work on the door. Rosamund wandered back over to the fire escape to make sure no one was following them. Now she was out on the roof and exposed to view, Gibraltar's warnings seemed much more real.

She first saw the helicopter coming around the bend of the river. It did not immediately catch her attention, for helicopters were common enough; just a news crew on a story, or an air ambulance heading for the hospital. This one was flying very low, but for some reason its landing lights were off, and Rosamund, who knew more about helicopters than most people, somehow noticed this. The helicopter was a V-27, a small fast passenger model just like the one she and Emily had owned themselves. She had seen and heard it landing dozens of times, and there was something about this particular machine, some note in the engine, that alerted her, even before she glimpsed the red letter $\mathcal{M}$ on the underbelly. As Rosamund took this in and realized what it must mean, the landing lights came on, and the machine swung over the building and began to descend.

"Gibraltar!" Rosamund began to run. "It's Operation Miniver! They've found us!"

The Land Rover had not been gone for more than a few minutes, and Fiona had barely seated herself in front of the television, when Livia came in. She shut the living-room door with a determined click and turned the TV off.

"Rosamund," she said. "What's she up to?"

One glance told Fiona she had been rumbled. She shrank back on the sofa and shook her head. Livia grabbed Fiona's shoulder and shook it.

"Tell me quickly. I saw Rosamund getting into the car; I know she's gone with Gibraltar, and I know you helped her. What's she trying to do?"

"I don't know!" Fiona cried. "Leave me be, you're hurting me!" She tried to pull her arm out of Livia's grip. They tussled a moment longer, and the door opened and Lindsey and Aunt Edie came in.

"What on earth's this?" exclaimed Lindsey.

Livia let go of Fiona's shoulder. "It's Rosamund. She's gone off with Gibraltar, and Fiona won't tell me what it's all about." Fiona rolled off the sofa on to the floor and edged away. Aunt Edie put a grandmotherly arm around her.

"There, there dear," she said soothingly. "Don't fret; nobody's going to hurt you. Livia's worried, that's all. Just tell us exactly what happened."

Lindsey looked hard at Fiona, who turned red and then white under her scrutiny. "Fiona? What's this about? Has Rosamund gone with Gibraltar?"

Fiona began to cry. She had helped Rosamund against her own better judgement, and to have all these adults demanding to know what was happening was simply dreadful. "I couldn't help it," she wept. "Rose asked me to smuggle her into the car; she wanted to go with him. What else was I supposed to do?"

"Say no, of course," said Livia immediately. "You silly girl. Why on earth did you do it?"

"Stop that," said Lindsey. "Fiona, let me get this straight. Rosamund has gone with Gibraltar to the Archives, and he doesn't know she's there? What exactly is she trying to do? She knows quite well he wanted to go alone."

"I don't know exactly what she was planning," said Fiona miserably. "I tried to tell her not to, but she's a Miniver. How could I possibly say no?"

Lindsey sighed. She understood better than anyone what Fiona must have gone through, for she was a fan herself. While half of her knew perfectly well that Rosamund was an irresponsible teenager, to the other half she would always be the miniature celebrity who had captured the hearts of a city. If the Minivers' magic still worked on her, with all her years and experience, it was hardly surprising that Fiona should have been unable to resist Rosamund's coaxing.

"Well," said Lindsey, "I'm sure Gibraltar will be able to work out what to do." She turned back to Livia, but the spot where she had been standing was unexpectedly empty. The French door was open and they heard an engine starting up outside.

Aunt Edie pulled back the curtains and gave a shout of alarm. "My car! Lindsey, that woman's stealing my car!"

The helicopter had reached the city. When the first tall office blocks came into view Ron dropped down and flew as low as he dared, following the curve of the river until they could all see the square of darkness that was the Archives building. Ron manoeuvred in close and snapped on *Emily-Rose's* landing lights. The helicopter hovered briefly over the flat rooftop, and slowly began to descend.

Emily took off her seatbelt. The City Archives was such a distinctive building that it was easy to identify even from the air, and she could see the roof below them through the cabin window. It was set on an angle to the street, and there was a strange pyramid-shaped skylight in the centre. Something appeared to be moving on the edge of the roof, a human figure, very small.

Emily gasped. "Ron! Rose and Gibraltar are down on the roof!"

"I can see them."

Millamant joined Emily at the window. They waved and banged on the glass, trying to catch Rosamund's attention, and though there was no way Rosamund could possibly have heard them, she looked up. Emily waved furiously. Rosamund squinted, and shaded her eyes with her arm to protect them from the glare of the landing lights. The helicopter's markings were so large and clear, she could not have missed them.

Then everything went wrong. Rosamund turned and started to run away, and Emily lost sight of her as she passed under the helicopter and out of her field of vision. She ducked across to the opposite window, and saw Rosamund disappear again around the nearest corner of the pyramid.

"Where's she going?"

Milly came up behind her. "Rose doesn't realize it's us. She doesn't know we've got the helicopter. She probably thinks it's Madame."

"We've got to stop them!" Emily jumped up and down. She banged on the window, doing everything she could to catch Rosamund's attention. But no amount of impatience could land the helicopter any faster, and though Emily was waiting to jump out the moment its skids touched on the roof, the delay had been enough. Apart from themselves, the roof was empty.

Rosamund and Gibraltar were gone.

10
THE PRIME MINISTER

Madame was thinking about the past.

It was something she did not do very often if she could help it. The past was full of too many painful memories. Madame's life had been a battlefield of failures and disappointments going back to when she was a little girl. She could not explain why this should be so. That it might have had something to do with herself would never have occurred to her.

"You never loved me," she said to the still figure lying on the bed in front of her. "You pretended you did, but I know you didn't."

Papa King made a noise between a grunt and a cry. The doctors had told Madame that, even though he could not speak himself, he could understand every word she said. His dark eyes, the only mobile thing in his face, tried to fix on hers, but Madame deliberately looked away.

"You sent us into exile," she said. "We had nothing to

live on. Nobody wanted anything to do with us; we were so poor we had to live in an old railway carriage. My mother went mad. Did you know that? By the end of her life, she didn't even know who I was. I had to look after her. There was no one else."

Papa King blinked. His eyes looked suspiciously moist, but Madame reminded herself that this meant nothing. She had been told by the doctor that stroke victims often cried for no reason at all. Papa King had not wept when she had been an unloved, lonely little girl. There had been no tears when he had ordered Madame and her mother to leave Artemisia for ever; in fact, he had not even said goodbye. As she sat at Papa King's bedside, looking at the machine ticking over his heartbeats, Madame recalled the day they had left. She remembered getting into the unmarked police car in the palace courtyard and looking up at the Walnut Office window. She had hoped for one last glimpse of Papa King, but he had not been there. There would be no last-minute forgiveness. As the car rolled out into the streets of Artemisia for what she had believed was the very last time, Madame had cursed her father from the bottom of her heart.

She had known then that things were bad, but she had not yet realized how truly desperate they would become. Nothing could have prepared her for the poverty and misery, and the sheer hopelessness of watching her life slowly ticking away. Yet Papa King had not even cared. He had found himself new daughters instead, the pretty and talented Miniver sisters, and he had left her to rot in exile and despair. Madame's heart flooded with rage at the thought. It was all Papa King's fault. If he had not sent her away, she would never have become involved with Titus; would never have trusted him to restore her stolen position; would never have listened to his lies. Well, it would not happen again. She would not let it. Madame's hand went to the machine that kept Papa King breathing. Her fingers gripped the plastic tubes that connected him to the oxygen cylinders by the bed. The flesh on her fingertips went white under the pressure. The plastic began to slip against the nozzle, and then suddenly, the phone on the bedside table rang.

Madame jumped back from the machine like a guilty schoolgirl. The phone shrilled again and she snatched it up.

"Hello?"

"A car is being sent for you." Titus's voice sounded strangely distorted down the line. "It will be at the palace in five minutes. I expect you to be waiting."

Madame's throat tightened as if she were drowning.

"I won't go. This is nothing to do with me. You can't make me do this."

"I can, and I will," Titus replied. "Be there. Because if you are not, secret documents will be read out that even the Parliament of Artemisia cannot ignore. Five minutes. I'll be expecting you."

He rang off. Madame put the receiver down with shaking hands. Secret documents. So it was true. He had found the Most Secret Room and she was totally in his power.

She thought she had never been so afraid of anyone as she was of Titus now.

Brenda Bertram had always been a failure. She was forty years old and not very clever; she had never held down a decent job, or owned a house, or done any of the things respectable people thought were important. Even Fiona's father had not stuck around long enough to see their daughter born. To her family, she had always been "Silly" or "Nutty" Brenda, or "Poor" Brenda if they happened to be feeling kind. Most of the time they weren't, but Brenda was used to this. The best she ever hoped for was that when Christmas Day came around, someone would remember to ask her and Fiona for lunch.

When Titus had told Brenda she was to become an

MP, her immediate reaction was to panic. Until now, the only job she had managed to hold down was some part-time work at the local greengrocer's, packing potatoes and runner beans in plastic bags. It was all very well for Holly to say that if she did what she was told she would have an office and lots of money, and limousines to take her wherever she wanted. Brenda had already been doing what Titus told her for some time, and so far all this had done was take Fiona away from her, and make her more frightened every day.

"Oh, for goodness' sake," snapped Holly, as Brenda fumbled in her handbag for a handkerchief and began to cry. They were waiting with Len on the front steps of the Artemisia Parliament, and the last thing she wanted was for Brenda to spoil things. "There's nothing to be worried about. Anyone would think you didn't want to be here."

"I don't," said Brenda, in a muffled voice. "I want to go home. I want Fiona."

Holly sighed. "Well, you can't have Fiona. And you can't go home until we've been sworn in. Pull yourself together. This is very important." As she spoke, Primrose came out of the parliament building and down the steps.

"Madame's just arrived at the back entrance," said Primrose. "We're ready now." She looked at Brenda, who was drying her eyes hastily in case Titus was somewhere nearby. "What's the matter with her?"

"Oh, nothing," said Holly in an exasperated voice. "Worrying about that wretched kid of hers."

"She'd better be quiet inside, or she'll have something to worry about," said Primrose, ominously. "Follow me."

Holly, Len and Brenda went up the front steps and into Parliament House. It was a beautiful building, with rich carpets and walls lined with old-fashioned portraits. As they passed the Members' Dining Room, they could smell something delicious cooking. Whenever Parliament sat, which was not often, the MPs had a roast dinner with crispy vegetables, and bread-and-butter pudding for dessert. For most of them, this was the really important part of the evening, and they raced as quickly as they could through their ten minutes of business in order to get to it.

There were no MPs around now. The only people Brenda saw as she climbed the marble stairs were guards wearing the light-blue shirts that had once belonged to the Minivers House Security Team, but which were now the uniform of Operation Miniver. If Fiona had been there, she would have pointed out to her mother that Operation Miniver was rapidly becoming Titus's private army. But Brenda was not clever enough to realize this by herself, and by the time she and her companions reached the impressive oak door of the parliamentary chamber, she was so frightened about the ceremony she had to get through that she barely wondered about the dozen guards who were standing in front of it.

"All ready, are we?" Titus came strolling up to them with Madame on his arm. If not for the fact that Madame was wearing black and had an expression as if she would rather be anywhere else than here, Brenda would have thought they looked rather like a bride and groom.

Primrose nodded. She stepped up the door and gestured for Brenda and the others to get out of the way. The dozen guards muscled together in a tight blue clump. On a signal from Titus, they charged the doors and burst through into the chamber beyond.

What followed happened in a kind of blur. Brenda, who was at the back of the group in the corridor, glimpsed several people inside the room jumping to their feet and trying to run away from the guards. She heard yells and shouts, and an old-ladyish sort of scream. There was a thud as something heavy was knocked over, and then Primrose could be heard, shouting, "Back to your seats! Back to your seats!" like an especially mean type of teacher. Titus wandered up to the open door and stood looking into the chamber with a satisfied expression. An old man was lying on the floor at his feet, just inside the doorway, though whether he had fainted or suffered something far worse, nobody particularly seemed to care.

The guards brought the situation quickly under control. When the noise had stopped and the elderly MPs had been forced back to their seats, Titus took Madame's arm again, stepped over the unconscious man and walked into the chamber. The rest of them followed. Brenda would have liked to do something for the man on the floor, but when she made as if to help him, Holly grabbed her arm and shoved her, stumbling, into the room.

A small group of old wrinkly people was sitting in leather chairs around a polished table. Their expressions were frightened and confused, but since the table where they sat was ringed by armed guards, this was hardly surprising. Titus escorted Madame up to the far end of the table, gripping her arm mercilessly when she tried to hold back. He was carrying a long, thin, folded piece of paper in his left hand, and when Madame looked as if she was going to rebel, he lifted it very slightly so she could see. The fight instantly went out of her. Madame leaned heavily on the lectern and spoke into the microphone.

"The oaths will now be taken."

Someone thrust a typewritten sheet into Brenda's hand. Prompted by Holly, she read through it with the others, hoping that no one else noticed how she stumbled over the big words. Brenda wasn't exactly sure what it all meant, but it was to do with serving the kingdom of Artemisia to the best of her ability, while the breath was still in her body. When they had finished, there was silence. Madame stood, clinging to the lectern, looking around the room as if she hoped someone would save her. She turned to Titus, but his forefinger tapped against the long folded document he was holding in his left hand, and Madame swallowed. With an effort, and in a thread of a voice that was scarcely audible even with the help of the microphone, she spoke.

"I, Karen, do hereby accept your oaths on behalf of my father, the King of Artemisia. I appoint you members for life of this Parliament and welcome you to this assembly."

Titus began to clap. The applause was so loud in the quiet chamber that Brenda almost jumped out of her best shoes. The security guards joined in and, after a moment, the ancient MPs put their hands together as well. The new members made their way to some empty chairs. Brenda found herself sitting next to Titus. Across the table, Holly was beaming.

Titus set the paper he was holding down on the table. "Thank you for your warm welcome. And now, since we're here, let's get down to business. First, I would like to move that Madame be known from now on as Karen, Princess of Artemisia."

"Seconded," said Len at once.

Madame opened her mouth. "I—"

Titus immediately cut her off. "Any objections? Motion carried. Go on, Princess Karen. Sit in the big chair, like a good girl."

Two security guards stepped forward and seized Madame by the arms. They dragged her to a chair, almost a throne, that was standing on a platform at the end of the room. It was carved out of ebony, with a high back and armrests shaped like liquorice twists. Madame struggled gracelessly for a moment, before plonking herself down on the velvet cushion. She looked as if she was about to cry with rage.

Another of the new MPs had risen to her feet.

"I move that Titus be appointed Prime Minister of Artemisia," said Holly loudly.

"Seconded!" piped up Len.

"Objections?"

Brenda opened her mouth, but a foot stamped down hard on hers under the table, and she gasped with pain instead. Titus smiled.

"Carried," he said. "I accept the appointment. And now—"

"Excuse me, sir."

The big doors of the chamber opened. A guard came hurrying in and whispered into Titus's ear. As Titus listened, a change came over his face. His slight, satisfied smile suddenly faded, his eyebrows drew together and he pushed back his chair and stood up.

"Ladies and gentlemen, excuse me, but I fear I must adjourn our proceedings." He jerked his head at Primrose, and at once walked out of the room.

Primrose followed. There was a brief silence, then a general stampede for the door. Holly, Len and the guards bolted after Titus, the old MPs seized the chance to run for their lives, and in less than half a minute, the chamber was almost deserted.

Sitting on her throne, an incredulous expression on her face, Madame suddenly found herself forgotten. Then she saw that the folded paper Titus had been holding was lying abandoned on the main table. Slightly wobbly in the high heels she had still not managed to get used to, she hurried over and snatched it up.

On the front, in black curly writing, were the words *LAST WILL AND TESTAMENT*. Madame's heart pumped so hard that for a moment she thought she was going to collapse. Her hands fumbled as she unfolded the single sheet. She turned it over, and then over again, until at last it crumpled and tore and she threw it with a shriek on to the table. Titus had been holding a blank will form, a piece of paper with nothing written on it at all. The paper was a fake.

Titus had used the oldest bluff in the book and she had fallen for it. Pure rage seized Madame, stronger than any emotion she had ever felt in her life. She kicked the table leg with her foot, yelled with pain, then snatched off her shoe and hurled it at the wall in fury. A little gasp off to her right caught her attention. Madame whirled around. There was one MP left, the new one with a face like a sheep, who had been sitting next to Titus.

"Where have they gone?" Madame demanded. "Come on. You were sitting right next to him. You must have heard what was said."

Brenda cringed like a mistreated dog. Madame grabbed a twist of her mousy hair and gave it a good hard yank.

"Idiot! Where have they gone?"

Brenda winced and squirmed. "He— He said there'd been a break-in. At the Archives. Please let me go! You're hurting me!"

"A break-in?" Madame stared, but there was nothing else Brenda could tell her. She gave Brenda's hair an extra tug for good measure, then looked around for the shoe she had thrown away. It had disappeared, so she kicked off the other impatiently and ran in her stockinged feet out of the room.

Madame sped down the marble staircase and out into the MPs' garden. It was famous for its roses, and the scent of the deep-red blossoms that had been planted in honour of her grandmother, Queen Rosamund, filled the air like a heavy incense. Beyond the wrought-iron fence a few people were going about their business, walking home from restaurants and cinemas along the city footpaths. A few passers-by recognized Madame's face and pointed, but Madame paid them no attention. Her stockings tore as she ran along the pavement, and she winced when she trod on something sharp, but there was only one thought in her head, and that was to get to the Archives before anything further went wrong.

When she arrived, the others had already gone inside, and the bronze doors were shut. Madame ran up the steps and banged on them with her fists.

"Let me in!"

There was a long delay. Madame kept banging on the door and eventually heard a key turning. A small door creaked open to her left and a face peeped out. It belonged to a young woman, surely the youngest and least important member of Operation Miniver, who had been left behind when the rest had gone inside the Archives. The name on her security tag was *Trudy Nicholls*.

"I'm sorry, the Archives are closed. I've been told I can't let anybody in. You can't—"

"I most certainly can," said Madame rudely. She

shoved her foot into the door, forgetting that she had no shoes on. The girl panicked and started to shut it, and as the door closed on Madame's foot she screamed and started hopping up and down. Trudy let go in fright. Madame half pushed, half fell through the open doorway. As soon as she was inside, she dealt the doorkeeper a ringing box over the ears.

"Where's Titus gone?"

"He's up on the roof," said Trudy, in a wavering voice. "A helicopter landed there about half an hour ago. I sent a message for him to come back urgently."

"I'm not interested in the helicopter," said Madame. "What's Titus been doing here? Where's he been working?"

"In Ms Milton's office," said Trudy. "He's been searching for some sort of secret room, but I don't think he's found it."

"Indeed," said Madame. "Well, if you know what's good for you, you'll take me straight up there. This time, Titus has overplayed his hand."

11
ASSAULT ON THE ARCHIVES

By the time the rotors on the helicopter had slowed and Emily had jumped out on to the Archives rooftop, any chance of catching up with Rosamund was past. Emily did not wait for the others, but ran straight to the place where she had seen her sister and Gibraltar disappear. There was a blue door there with a splintered edge. It had been left ajar, and Emily pushed it open to reveal a metal staircase going down into the depths of the building.

"*Rose? Are you there?*" Emily set her foot on the first step. She would have gone further, but someone grabbed her under the armpits and swung her bodily back through the door. She was dropped in a heap on the concrete roof, and the person who had caught her up hastily positioned himself between her and the door. Emily looked up and saw that it was Ron.

"What did you do that for?" Emily was furious. "Rose has gone down there. We've got to find her."

"No, we don't," replied Ron. "We came to the Archives to find the Most Secret Room, not your sister. I don't know what Rosamund is doing here, but we need to finish the job we planned to do first."

"I want to find Rose," said Emily stubbornly. "She might be in danger."

"Rosamund is in no more danger than we are," said Ron. "We don't know where she is. She may be in the building, but it's a very big place. We could wander around for hours and not find out where she is."

"Ron's right, Emmie," said Millamant. "First things first. Rose has got Gibraltar with her. I'm sure she'll be all right."

"I hope so." Emily knew when she was outvoted, but she had not expected this setback, and could not help feeling anxious about what Rosamund was doing. It was not a good way to start their mission. Ron helped her to her feet, and Milly reached for her hand. With Ron leading the way, they went through the door Gibraltar had forced and found themselves at the top of a set of metal steps. The stairwell was lit by several safety lights, and at the bottom was another door which had been locked, but which someone else had forced.

"Looks like they're definitely inside," said Ron, in a low voice. "Let's be careful. We don't know who else might be around."

He peeped around the door to check there was no one watching and the three of them crept out into a dreary-looking corridor. It was lined with chipped and badly painted doors that all looked the same, and all were locked tightly shut. Emily guessed they were offices, but there was nothing to tell them who worked inside. At the end of the corridor, another passage led away at right angles. A water cooler hummed quietly in an alcove, but otherwise it looked exactly like the first.

"We need to go this way." Millamant led them along the passage and turned into yet another identical corridor. It did not take Emily long to realize that there was no way she would be able to find Rosamund in this building. There were simply too many passages, too many doors and rooms to disappear into. Emily tried not to worry about it, but the fact that Rose was somewhere close by was a constant distraction. What on earth were she and Gibraltar doing here? Were they, too, looking for the Most Secret Room? It was hard to imagine how they expected to find it if they were. As they traced their way down a staircase and along even more featureless passages, Millamant abruptly stopped. She turned and looked back in the direction from which they had come, and screwed up her plain little face in a confused pucker.

"Oh, dear," she said. "I think we need to be another

level down. Either that, or they've changed the layout of the building. I'm sorry. It's a long time since I've worked here."

"Take your time," urged Ron. "We mustn't make a mistake."

"I don't know." Millamant turned and looked first one way, and then the other. They heard the sound of footsteps coming up the stairs.

"Quick." Ron grabbed a handle and wrenched open a door. Unfortunately, it was a broom cupboard. There was a clatter as something fell over, and Emily found herself with her bottom in a mop bucket and a broom tickling her face. Ron pulled the door to close it, but it did not quite shut. They all held their breath. Through the tiny gap in the door Emily saw several people hurrying towards them down the corridor.

There were about half a dozen security guards, and Titus was with them, unfamiliar in a smartly cut suit. Emily felt certain that somebody must notice them, but no one did. The group passed by, turned the corner and was gone. Ron waited a moment longer, then opened the door and stepped out into the hall.

"Heading for the roof," he said. "They must be going to secure the helicopter. Well, I suppose it was too much to hope they wouldn't notice it. It's going to make getting away a lot more difficult, but we'll deal with that problem when we come to it. Millamant, do you know where we're going yet?"

Millamant pointed back in the direction of the staircase. "That way. The Archivist's office was above the main reading room. We need to go down another floor."

They all trooped back and went down the stairs. Emily whispered into Millamant's ear.

"Are you sure you remember where the Most Secret Room was?"

"As long as we find the City Archivist's office." Millamant nodded. "Ah. This looks better. That's the office, over there."

Any hope Emily had nursed that Rosamund and Gibraltar might have been there before them was immediately dashed, for the Archivist's door was secured by a padlock. Ron forced it with his chisel. The sound of the metal giving way seemed to echo down the deserted passage, and Emily felt her heart pound with nervous excitement. They were so close now. If they could only get into the Most Secret Room and find the will, then their problems might at last be over.

"Goodness," said Millamant, as Ron switched on the lights. "Somebody's made a right mess in here. What on earth have they been up to?"

The three of them stood, looking around. Emily had not been sure what to expect of the Archivist's office, but it was certainly not this wreck of a room, with the carpets ripped up and everything dropped piecemeal on the floorboards. Someone had ripped most of the plaster off the walls and ceiling, and there was rubble everywhere. Emily dragged a chunk of fallen plaster off a heap. A white cloud flew up and enveloped her and she fell back, coughing.

"This will be Titus's doing," Ron said. "I wonder if he's found anything? It looks as if he knew the Most Secret Room was here somewhere, but wasn't exactly sure where."

"The entry was in the floor." Millamant walked to the middle of the room and looked around, as if getting her bearings. "There was a sort of trapdoor in the back corner, and a staircase going down. I don't think the actual room was very big. It was more like a cupboard, set into the outside stone wall of the building."

Ron scanned the floor. "Well, they've taken all the carpet up, but I can't see anything that looks like a trapdoor. If there was one, I'm sure Titus would have found it."

"There's a door over here." Emily wandered over to the corner and strained on tiptoe to reach the door handle. Millamant frowned.

"This is nothing like I remember." She took a step forward and spun around to face the back corner. Then she began to pace across the room, counting under her breath.

"I'm right. I'm sure I'm right. The office was never this shape when old Kennedy was the Archivist. It's much narrower, and that wall" – Millamant pointed – "I'm sure that wall wasn't there. Somebody's put in a partition. The Most Secret Room must be on the other side."

"Where's Emily gone?" said Ron, suddenly. Millamant turned. The door in the partition wall was open and Emily had vanished. As Millamant and Ron looked at each other, there was a blood-curdling scream from the next room. . .

Safe in the knowledge that Titus and the guards were up on the roof, Madame had frogmarched the guard, Trudy, up the main stairs to Glenda Milton's office. She had not expected to find anybody there, and had been surprised when she heard lowered voices talking on the other side of the door. Madame could not make out how many people were inside, nor could she identify the speakers, but she supposed that they must be members of Operation Miniver. Perhaps Titus had left guards there, just in case.

Madame felt enormously frustrated. After months of

searching for the Most Secret Room, she finally had a real clue as to its whereabouts; yet she could not get into the Archivist's office. There was, however, another door to the left of Glenda Milton's, and this had been left slightly ajar. Madame pushed it open. With Trudy still in tow, she crept into what looked like an office designed for the Archivist's assistant.

Madame did not dare turn on the lights in case somebody saw her, but in the glow that filtered through from the corridor she could just make out a desk and, at the other end of the room, a second door which obviously opened on to the main office. She was standing, wondering what to do next, when the handle on this inner door gave a sinister rattle and began to turn.

Behind her, Trudy gasped. Madame grabbed the girl's wrist and dug her fingernails into the flesh as a kind of warning. The door rattled again and the handle wriggled back and forth. With a creak, the door swung open and a small white figure glided into the room.

Until this moment, Madame had never been sure whether she believed in ghosts. Before she had turned completely crazy, her mother, Susan, had gone through a phase of claiming to be a medium. She had held regular seances in their railway carriage which had been attended by all sorts of strange people. Some of the seances had been very creepy, but most of the time nothing had happened, and Madame had remained unconvinced. But now, in front of her, was proof that the dead walked. Madame screamed.

"What do you want of me?" she cried hoarsely. "Why are you here?"

The ghost shook its head violently. It was wearing the same grubby clothes Emily Miniver had been dressed in when Madame had last seen her, but they were now streaked a spectral white. Its eyes were dark and grim in a dead white face, and when it opened its mouth, it spoke in a small hard voice.

"You tried to kill me."

Madame turned pale as a ghost herself. Her legs shook and she dropped to her knees with shock. It was said that the unquiet dead returned to revenge themselves on their killers. Had the spirit of the murdered Emily come to drag her down to another world?

"Don't hurt me!" she wept. "Please, please, have mercy! I didn't mean it. It wasn't me, it was Ron. Ron killed you, not me!"

"Did someone call my name?" said a voice, and Ron's sandy, unghostly head popped around the door. The ghost turned and Madame noticed that the back of its T-shirt was not nearly as white as the front. Her eyes narrowed, and she jumped to her feet. Ron grabbed the ghost's shoulder and defensively pushed her behind him. In that moment, everything became clear.

"Traitor!" screeched Madame. "*Traitor!*"

She lunged forward, and there was an explosive crack that turned everything upside down. For a fleeting instant, Madame felt as if she was flying through space. A bright light flashed behind her eyes and then with a thud she was lying on the floor with her lips pressed against the carpet.

The security guard, Trudy, had come up behind and coshed her on the head.

As soon as they had seen the helicopter, Rosamund and Gibraltar had known there was likely to be trouble. Whoever was at the controls would certainly have seen them, and was very likely to follow. There was also every chance that the pilot would alert anyone inside the building to go and look for them. Gibraltar had counted on finding Titus alone, but once he heard of their arrival, it was going to be very hard to manage this. Their only hope was to get deep inside the building as quickly as possible, and use Gibraltar's local knowledge to keep out of sight of their pursuers.

Gibraltar led Rosamund down a narrow staircase, used only by staff. She was grateful that he seemed to know exactly where he was going, because it soon appeared that the Archives had as many tiny passageways and back staircases as an ant heap. After many twists and turns, and constant checking behind and ahead of them, they emerged into the gallery walkway that led around the top of the reading room. Rosamund stood for a moment, looking through the polished banisters into the space below. It was unlit, but a dim glow filtered in from the building's grand entrance, and it was just possible to make out the shadowy outlines of what looked like hundreds of desks.

"There," said Gibraltar. He crouched beside Rosamund and pointed. "Over there, behind that column. That desk was my regular spot for about six or seven years."

Rosamund nodded. She leaned her forehead against the banisters and tried to think back into the past, when Millamant had worked at the Archives as a cleaner, and Gibraltar had been writing his books. She closed her eyes, and for a moment, it felt as if the reading room was full of ghosts. She saw Gibraltar and Millamant as their younger selves; Madame and Susan and Papa King; and going back even further, Papa King's mother, the original Queen Rosamund, for whom she had been named. But when she opened her eyes and looked down again, Rosamund saw that the room was still empty, and there was no sign even of Operation Miniver. Under the circumstances, this seemed surprising. But when Rosamund mentioned it to Gibraltar, he shook his head.

"It's a very big building," he said. "There are three storeys above ground, and nine basements below. How many people are working for Operation Miniver? Twenty? Twenty-five?"

"There were eighteen guards in our security team," said Rosamund. "If you add in Titus and the other members of the club committee there'd be a few more. I suppose that's not very many, but when they're all out to get you, it feels like an army."

"The only person who really matters is Titus," said Gibraltar. "The others won't hurt us. We just need to keep out of their way."

Gibraltar stood up. Rosamund followed him obediently out of the gallery and down the stairs. She was not sure where she had expected him to go looking for Titus, but she soon realized that they were heading into the basements. This was something Rosamund had not expected, and a feeling of reluctant dread started seeping through her. When she had first gone on the run from Madame, Gibraltar had been working at the

Archives as a porter. He had hidden her in the basements for several days, and Rosamund had never been in a more loathsome or frightening place.

The first few levels were unpleasant, but not unbearable. They were filled with the most commonly used files, and there were lights in the walls and offices, where the archivists worked like moles among the stacks of decaying paper. But Rosamund's feeling of anxiety grew as they continued downwards, and her sharp Miniver ears kept straining at tiny sounds, until she was almost convinced that they were being followed. When they reached the fourth level, Rosamund was no longer in any doubt. Something was definitely happening that she had not been told about.

"Gibraltar?" she asked in a small voice. "What are we doing? Surely we're not going to find Titus down here?"

Gibraltar was walking slightly ahead of Rosamund. She saw him pause mid-step. His shoulders stiffened slightly and he swung back to face her.

"No," he admitted. "We're not. I'm sorry, Rose, but it all stops here for you. I told you tonight would be dangerous, but I don't think you really understood. If you're there when I speak to Titus, he'll probably kill you. For everyone's sake, I can't let that happen."

From Gibraltar's expression, Rosamund could tell that there was no protest she could make that he would listen to. Nevertheless, despite the fact that she had come against his instructions, she still felt betrayed. At last she managed a reply.

"That's not fair. I'm not a coward, Gibraltar."

Gibraltar squatted down so he was at her level. 'I know you're not, Rose," he said, in a troubled tone. "But your being here is not going to help, and it could ruin everything. Please, do as I ask. I want you to hide down here in one of the offices, and when everything is over, I'll come back and fetch you. Here, I'm going to give you my watch. If I'm not back in two hours, I want you to get out of this building in whatever way you can."

He unclipped his watch and handed it to her. It was so huge, Rosamund could have wrapped it around her leg and had room to spare. She put it silently on her left arm and shoved it up underneath her sleeve. Her eyes were burning with held-back tears, but whether they were from fear or disappointment she could not have told. She had a terrible foreboding that she would never see Gibraltar again.

It seemed too difficult to say goodbye, so she merely watched as he went off down the corridor, leaving her in a darkened office with only the glow from outside to see by. When he had faded from sight, Rosamund sat down on the concrete floor and wondered how she would ever get through the next two hours. According to the watch, it was nearly ten o'clock, and she wondered what was happening back at Aunt Edie's. It would be too much to expect that Lindsey and the others would not have noticed her disappearance, and she hoped that Fiona had not got into too much trouble on her account.

"Well, look what we have here."

Rosamund started. A plump woman with thin blonde hair was standing in the doorway of the office. Rosamund immediately recognized Primrose, the security guard who had so eagerly turned against her and Emily when their fortunes changed. In the days when they had been famous, Primrose had always been Rosamund's least favourite bodyguard. She had always sensed that Primrose resented her job, and now she had Rosamund cornered, the expression on her face was one of gloating nastiness.

"Little Princess Rosamund. You don't look much of a princess now, do you? Sitting down here in the dark like a trapped rat, hoping nobody will find you."

Rosamund did not reply. She was too proud to show that she was frightened, but in fact, Primrose's unexpected appearance had scared her so much she was almost paralysed. Reminding herself she was a Miniver, and probably the next Queen of Artemisia, she stayed where she was and looked up with what she hoped was as expression of haughty indifference. Naturally,

Primrose wasn't fooled. She grinned and reached down to grab hold of Rosamund's arm.

"Up you get, princess." The yank she gave Rosamund's wrist almost lifted her off the floor. "Don't seem anything very special now, do you? No, stop that struggling. You know you're not going anywhere."

There was no point in fighting, but Rosamund did it anyway. She scored a well-aimed kick on Primrose's ankle, which would have been more effective if she'd been wearing harder shoes; then ducked her head and tried to bite the fingers gripping her wrist. Her teeth sank into her attacker's flesh, and Primrose swore. She dealt Rosamund a backhanded clip over the ear and they grappled a moment longer. It was a hopelessly unequal struggle, but Rosamund was strong and wiry enough to plant a few more desperate kicks on Primrose's shins.

"Help! Someone help!" Out of the corner of her eye, Rosamund saw something moving in the corridor behind Primrose. Gibraltar had heard the struggle and was coming back, but rescue was a miracle she could not take for granted. Primrose was armed, and Gibraltar was alone; she had to keep Primrose distracted. It was your eyes that did it. She had to not look at him; she had to keep her gaze on Primrose and not give Gibraltar away. . .

Rosamund gave a sudden scream and went limp in

Primrose's grip. "Ow!" she cried. "Ow, ow, ow!"

Taken off guard, Primrose let Rosamund drop to the floor. As she did, one strong hand seized the back of her collar, and a second grabbed the gun from the holster at her belt. Rosamund rolled away triumphantly and jumped to her feet. Gibraltar was standing before them both, holding the gun.

Primrose stared at him resentfully. "You're not going to use that."

"Probably not," said Gibraltar. "Still, I have it, and you don't. Rose, frisk her and check her pockets."

Rosamund went over and felt in Primrose's pockets. She found a wallet, a packet of chewing gum, and a second gun loaded with tranquilizer darts.

"I suppose you've come to find out what Titus is doing," said Primrose, as Rosamund took these items from her. "Either that, or you're looking for your sister. Well, don't waste your time. There's something you don't know, Rose. Emily is dead."

"I don't believe you," said Rosamund. She knew it would have been better to have left the words unspoken, but she could not help them. "If Emily was dead, I'd know."

"Oh yes, the famous Minivers' magic bond," jeered Primrose. "Seems like it's not all it's cracked up to be, doesn't it?"

"She's baiting you, Rosamund," said Gibraltar. "Don't

listen."

"Of course she wants to listen," said Primrose. "Shall I tell you exactly what happened, Rosamund? It was Ron who did it. Madame told him he had to, because Emily was getting to be a nuisance. He gave her some kind of injection, and the poison stopped her heart. We put her body in a cardboard box and buried her out in the forest. I was there when it happened. I dug the hole."

Rosamund lost control. Later, when she had a chance to think about it, she realized it was the mention of the cardboard box which had done it, for while everything else Primrose had told them could easily have been said out of malice, it was the sort of detail that sounded like it might be true. She made a running leap at Primrose, and would have clawed her face to shreds if Gibraltar had not seized and held her back. Several seconds followed during which Rosamund could not make up her mind whether she was attacking Primrose or Gibraltar. Since the gun was still in his other hand, it took all Gibraltar's efforts to hold her back, and while they tussled briefly in the enclosed space, Primrose jumped to her feet. She darted through the office door. Gibraltar made a last desperate grab to catch her collar. Her blue shirt slipped between his fingers and she was gone.

The two of them followed her out into the corridor.

Primrose was nowhere to be seen, though whether she had gone up or down the nearby stairs, or had stayed on the same level, there was no way of telling. Gibraltar went over to the staircase. While Rosamund watched, he took the bullets out of Primrose's gun and dropped them in a scatter over the railing into the central well. When he tossed the gun after them, it seemed to take for ever to fall. He and Rosamund stood together, waiting by the railing, and at last, they heard the faintest clatter and then nothing.

"It's a long way down," remarked a voice.

They turned, and saw Titus smiling at them.

"I believe you wanted to speak with me?" he said.

12

TITUS TRIUMPHANT

When Livia left Aunt Edie's, she had not really been sure
what she was doing. She had been upset and very angry
with Rosamund, but most of all she had been frightened.
She had seen disaster looming, a disaster caused by
Rosamund's wilful behaviour. When it struck, it would
be the ruin of all of them. The others might sit waiting at
Aunt Edie's until the catastrophe hit, but Livia was not
going to hang around until their enemies came to get
her. The Minivers might have ruined her life, but she
was not going to let them destroy it.

There were no police cars on the road to the Archives.
If there had been, Livia would certainly have been
arrested for speeding. She drove wildly, and the fact that
Aunt Edie's car had manual gears, which she was not
used to, did not help. Luckily, by the time Livia reached
the city it was getting late, and there was not much traffic
on the streets. Livia did not even look for a parking
place, but drove up on to the footpath outside the

Archives and screeched to a halt in the courtyard at the front of the building.

Livia jumped out of the car and ran up the steps. The bronze doors were closed for the night, and for the first time it occurred to her that she might have trouble getting into the building. But while the main doors were firmly shut, a little crack of light shone around the jamb of the staff door to the left, and when Livia pushed, she found that it was open. The lights in the vaulted entrance hall were all on, and though the reading room beyond was in darkness, it was obvious that someone was in the building.

Livia went into the reading room, where the darkness lent a kind of camouflage. As soon as she found herself inside, she was hit by a wave of unexpected panic. There was something about the atmosphere in the Archives that made her spirits sink whenever she entered the building; something closed-in and terrifying that crushed her sense of who she was and made her feel dead and unimportant. Livia knew she should find Gibraltar as quickly as possible, but she did not know where he might be, or what she would say to him when she found him. By now he had presumably discovered that Rosamund had stowed away in the car. For the first time, Livia could not help wondering whether she would have been better off leaving him to deal with her in his own manner. She even had an uneasy feeling that she herself might not be welcome, either.

There were lights on in the upper levels of the building. Livia could see their glow filtering down the main staircase at the far end of the reading room, and since it seemed likely that this was where Gibraltar was, she began feeling her way in their direction. She was about halfway across the room when she saw a lone figure descending the stairs from the upper gallery. The light caught its fair hair, and Livia shrank down swiftly beside a desk where she could not be seen.

The man was carrying a walkie-talkie. A woman was talking to him, and though her words were distorted, they were loud enough for Livia to catch something of the sense of what she was saying. The speaker seemed to be a security guard, who was following somebody down into one of the basements. She was asking the man to join her, and he was apparently on his way, for when he reached the bottom of the stairs, he disappeared through the swing doors that led to the back workroom where the staff had access to the basement staircase and the document lifts.

Livia had never met Titus. Nevertheless, from his age and the fact that he was not wearing a security uniform, she felt quite sure she had just seen him. It was a little surprising that he was alone, but this would also make it easier to trail him. If Livia did that, the chances were Titus would lead her to Gibraltar, for she could not think who else the intruder in the basement might be. Livia fingered the key hanging around her neck. She made up her mind, stood up and began to follow.

The moment Madame hit the floor, Ron was at her side, feeling for a pulse. He lifted her eyelids, quickly checked for broken bones, and rolled her into a recovery position. Madame's head moved slightly, and Emily saw that there was blood in her hair where Trudy had hit her. She gave a little groan and her eyelids fluttered. Ron sat back on his haunches and turned to Emily.

"It's all right," he said. "She's only stunned, and not very badly. I expect she'll come to quite quickly. I certainly don't think she'll suffer any lasting harm."

"I'm awfully sorry, sir," said Trudy. She was still clutching the little rubber cosh she had used to knock Madame out. It was clear she had not worked out that Ron had switched sides. "I didn't mean to hurt her, honestly. Will I – will I get into awful trouble?"

"Not if I have anything to do with it," said Ron, glancing sideways to let Emily know she was not to give him away. "You were trained to protect the Minivers,

Trudy. That's exactly what you did. We're very grateful you kept your head. Perhaps you can explain exactly what's been happening? Madame was supposed to be at Parliament House tonight, with Titus. What is she doing here?"

"She came back," said Trudy. "When I saw the helicopter land, I didn't realize it was you, sir. I was all alone in the building, so I phoned through a message to Titus. He came straight here, and Madame followed him."

"Yes, we saw Titus on the way in, heading for the roof," said Ron. "He had half a dozen security guards with him. Do you know where the rest are?"

"Two were sent here, sir – Titus told them to check the door was still locked; you must have just missed them. And he sent Primrose to secure the basements. The rest were told to search the building."

"Good." Ron nodded, and Emily saw him weighing up the situation in his head. When they had decided to come to the Archives, they had gambled on the building being deserted. That would have given them a little window in which to act and make a swift getaway. Now, Titus would set a guard on their helicopter and, with the rest of Operation Miniver searching the building, their way back to the roof would certainly be blocked. There was only one other way out, through the front entrance.

That would be locked or guarded, too. With a sinking feeling, Emily realized that they were trapped inside the building. What made it even worse was that Rosamund and Gibraltar were trapped as well.

There was a little tap on the inner door and Millamant's face peeped around the jamb. "Is it safe? Can I come in yet?" She took a few steps into the room and recoiled when she saw Madame lying on the floor. "Goodness. What's *she* doing here?"

"Trying to find the Most Secret Room, I suppose," said Ron. He turned to Trudy. "Trudy, I want you to go up to the roof. Titus will have left a team to watch over the helicopter, but he won't wait around himself when he realizes there's no one there. Tell the guards that the emergency is over, take them all down to the front entrance, and wait for further orders. If you find any other members of Operation Miniver on the way, tell them to wait at the front entrance, too. Look smart, girl!" As Trudy hurried from the room intent on her instructions, he shut the door and spoke quickly to Emily and Millamant.

"We've got to get out of here before someone finds us. If that girl does as she's told, there's just a chance that the way back to the helicopter will be clear. If we hurry, we might be able to make it out of the building. I'm sorry, but the Most Secret Room will have to wait."

"But it's right here!" protested Millamant. "Here, in this room. Ron, we can't go now. I've finally worked out what's happened. This office used to be part of the main one, but someone has put in a wall." She pointed to the wall with the door. "The entrance to the Most Secret Room will be in this room, not the other one. That's why Titus couldn't find it." She started pulling at the carpet in the back corner. "It's in this corner somewhere. There's a section of floor that lifts up. It's very cleverly done: you wouldn't even realize it was there—"

"No." Ron spoke as a man accustomed to giving orders. "Stop right there. We don't have time. We don't even have the key; we'd have to break in, and then we'd need to pick out one document among hundreds. Finding Papa King's will is no use at all, if it gets us caught by Titus. I'm sorry, but we have to leave, *now*."

Emily felt like bursting into tears. She could not believe that they had come within a trapdoor's width of finding the Most Secret Room, only to give up now. Millamant's face was locked into a stubborn scowl. For a moment, Emily thought she was going to refuse to leave, but whatever else she might be, Millamant was never reckless. She moved obediently away from the corner, and accompanied Ron and Emily to the door. As they passed through into the corridor, Emily tugged at Ron's trousers, and when he bent down, summoned up the courage to whisper the question she had been longing to ask.

"What about Rose and Gibraltar?"

"I'm afraid we can't help them," said Ron. "Whatever happens now is up to them."

As soon as the door closed on Emily and her friends, Madame opened her eyes and sat up. Her head reeled and for a moment she did not know which way was up and which was down, but she was perfectly conscious and had been for some time. Ron had been right: she had been hurt, but not badly stunned. When he had sent Trudy up on to the roof to get the guards out of the way, Madame had already been waking up, and when Millamant had spoken about the location of the Most Secret Room, she had heard every single word. Indeed, it had been all she could do not to scream with joy and excitement.

Now, though her head was swimming and her legs were wobbly, nothing could have kept her from getting up. Madame staggered over to the desk and fished around in the drawers until she found a penknife. It took her some time to open the blade, for her eyes kept sliding in and out of focus, but she persisted until she had managed. Madame went down on her hands and knees and ran the knife blade under the edge of the carpet, in the corner where Millamant had claimed the Most Secret Room was hidden. Her head still hurt, but her focus was improving, and when she succeeded finally in prising the carpet away from the nails that held it to the floor, it was a relatively easy matter to fold it back, along with its rubber underlay. There were ancient-looking wooden floorboards underneath, but no sign of any obvious trapdoor. Madame thought back and tried to remember exactly what Millamant had said.

"It was very cleverly built," she murmured. "You wouldn't even realize it was there. A section of floorboards. . ." She ran her hands over the boards, and her finger snagged on what seemed to be a knothole in the wood. Madame stopped. She bent as close as she could, and with trembling fingers, pushed her knife into a tiny gap. . .

A bit of blackened wood shot out of the hole and Madame let out a shriek of triumph. She had discovered a keyhole; a keyhole that someone had carefully carved into the floor, and concealed with a tiny plug of wood. She had done it at last. After months of searching, she had found what Livia and Titus and everyone else had failed to discover. She was literally sitting on the doorstep of the Most Secret Room.

There was now only one remaining problem.

Madame did not have the key.

Livia had not expected to find following Titus difficult. She knew the Archives better than anyone else alive, for not only had she spent several years working there; when she had been searching for the Most Secret Room, she had mapped almost every inch of it. But from the moment they started to go down the stairs to the basements, the gap between her and Titus widened, and it soon occurred to Livia that she was going to have trouble keeping up.

Titus was already out of sight, at least a floor below her. If he got too far ahead, she would lose him in the darkness. Then she heard voices whispering, and realized that Titus had met someone else coming up the stairs from the lower basements, probably the woman who had spoken to him earlier on the walkie-talkie. Their conversation was brief, and Livia guessed Titus was giving orders. He went on alone, and the guard, whom Livia had heard Titus addressing as Primrose, sat down on the stairs half a flight below where Livia was standing, completely blocking her path.

Livia could not believe her bad luck. But after four or

five minutes, during which she almost made up her mind to sneak away, Primrose stood up and continued quietly down the stairs. Hugging the wall, and trusting the shadows to hide her, Livia followed. There was no sign of Titus or Gibraltar, but Primrose was moving so stealthily that Livia was sure she must be trying to creep up on someone. At the next bend in the staircase, she saw who it was. Rosamund Miniver was standing alone at the top of the next flight down, staring through the metal railings at something or someone on a lower level.

If anything had ever made Livia wonder why she had come, it was her reaction at this moment. Rosamund was so preoccupied with whatever she was watching that she had neither seen nor heard Primrose coming down the stairs behind her. She was defenceless, and Livia knew that, at the very least, she should shout a warning. Yet she was never closer to running away than she was at that moment, and was still struggling to decide how she should react when Rosamund spun unexpectedly around. With the smooth grace of a trained dancer, she whipped out a small silver gun she had been hiding in the folds of her shirt and shot Primrose in the stomach.

Primrose stopped in her tracks and pitched over on to the concrete floor. She was not dead, for the gun was the sort that fired tranquilizer darts and there was a small black dart sticking out of her stomach. But the shock of finding that Rosamund not only did not need rescuing, but had probably saved her from being caught herself, had been so great that Livia went weak at the knees. Her shout of warning turned into a limp squeak of shock. She stumbled down the last few steps and sat down in a rush at the bottom. Rosamund lowered the dart gun and looked up at her.

"I can't tell you how much I enjoyed doing that," she said matter-of-factly. "What are you doing here? Did you change your mind and decide to help Gibraltar after all?"

Since this was precisely what Livia had done, there was no reason why this remark should have annoyed her as much as it did. Yet, to admit that it was true was to acknowledge that Rosamund had not only been right to go running after Gibraltar, but that she been braver than Livia in doing it first. All Livia's old dislike of Rosamund came bubbling back. She pointed to the gun in Rosamund's hand and said, nettled, "Where did you get that from?"

"I took it off Primrose." Rosamund's expression grew suddenly grave. "Gibraltar and Titus have gone down into the lower levels. When Gibraltar told Titus he wanted to talk to him, Titus just headed off down the stairs and Gibraltar followed. I don't know what's happening. It's so dark down there I can't even see where they've gone."

Livia stared down the stairwell. She and Rosamund were now on the fourth level. She had always hated going down into the lower basements, and could not understand why anyone would enter them willingly. "Why did they even go down there?"

"To be private," said Rosamund. "They didn't want me to hear whatever it is that Gibraltar wants to tell Titus. It's to do with Titus's parents. I heard Gibraltar say that, and I don't think Titus liked it."

"His parents?" Livia's misgivings deepened. "In that case, why didn't they just send you away? They could easily be private up here; there's no need to go deeper. It's terrible down there."

"I know." Rosamund faltered. "Livia, I think Gibraltar's in danger. I could tell he thought so, too, but he went anyway. Do you think— Do you think we should go after them?"

Livia went over to the stairs and gripped the metal railing. She had brought with her a little torch she had found in Aunt Edie's glovebox, but the darkness in the lower basements was so complete she knew that its glow would scarcely reach past her own toes. Everything in her head said that her first instinct, that morning at the breakfast table, had been right. Gibraltar had taken a terrible and unacceptable risk in coming here, and she had been a fool to follow him. But as they stood at the top of the stairs, looking down into the darkness she had hoped never to revisit, Livia's emotions swamped her yet again. She could not bear to think of anything happening to Gibraltar, any more than she could stand the thought of Rosamund going ahead without her. She would not be proved a coward, not now, when she had come so far.

Livia flicked on the torch. "Come on."

They hurried downstairs together. Livia regretted her decision immediately. Each basement was progressively darker, warmer and more unpleasant, and Aunt Edie's torch was not much use, for it was not just small, but had batteries that were nearly flat as well. Livia knew it was more likely to warn Titus of their approach than to light their way, but as they sweated their way deeper into the building, she could not bring herself to turn it off. Rosamund's silence and the sound of her quick, anxious breathing told Livia that Rosamund was just as frightened as she was.

"Seven." Rosamund read the number on the concrete wall. The seventh basement was as deep into the Archives as most people had ever gone, and was the last level where there were any real records. There were a few old footprints, but the dust on the landing had recently been disturbed. It hung in the air and made Rosamund cough, and when Livia shone her puny torch over the floor, they saw the tracks where Titus and Gibraltar had passed.

Livia's face sagged. "Oh, surely not . . ." Her torchlight wavered over the makeshift stairs that led down to the eighth basement. There was no doubt that this was where Titus and Gibraltar had headed, but Livia could not understand why. There was nothing down there, only empty walls and darkness so thick you could almost taste it. The last time she had been there, Livia had been so frightened that she had run away.

In silence, she and Rosamund crept down the rickety stairs. For some time, Livia had been sweating and trembling, and her hand was slippery on the railing. The darkness was so intense that Livia felt as if it would crush her. As they neared the bottom of the flight she could hear voices not far ahead. Gibraltar was speaking to Titus, but his deep voice was disguised by echoes, and she could not make out the words.

"What is he saying?"

Rosamund listened intently. Miniver ears, though small, were sharp. "He's telling Titus to go back to his father. They're arguing. Oh, Livia, I'm frightened! What should we do?"

But Livia did not know. Her legs were shaking so much she could barely move, and the light from her torch seemed to be fading to the point where she could see neither floor nor walls. It was like being buried alive. Rosamund's fingers gripped at the hem of her skirt and together they inched past an intersection in the corridor. The quarrelling voices grew louder. They saw a dim glow, like another torch, and heard scuffling followed by a thud. Rosamund let go of Livia's skirt and broke into a run.

"*Gibraltar!*"

They had reached the intersection. Livia, who knew what lay ahead, stood frozen to the spot. She saw the gaping hole in the floor, the crooked number 9 on the wall with its arrow pointing downwards. And she saw Titus attacking Gibraltar, while Rosamund Miniver ran unheeding into the midst of the fight.

Titus looked up and saw Rosamund. Livia saw his face burning with fury; saw his lunge as Rosamund ran towards him; saw Gibraltar come between them. The two men grappled for a moment on the edge of the drop to the ninth and final basement. Titus's foot flashed out. It connected with Gibraltar's leg, hooking him off balance and the bigger man lost his footing and began to fall.

"*Gibraltar!*" In the horror of the instant, Livia scarcely knew whether it was she who had screamed his name or Rosamund. Gibraltar teetered on the edge of the hole in the floor. Then, with a final shove from Titus, he plunged through it, and the battery in Livia's torch failed completely, and the light went out.

The seconds that followed were complete confusion. Livia started forward and blundered into a wall. She could hear Rosamund yelling and guessed she had been caught by Titus, but there was nothing she could do, for the darkness was so complete she was unable to get her bearings. Livia stumbled around, tripped, and bumped into another wall. Someone cannoned into her legs and she screamed. It took her a moment to realize from the person's height it must be Rosamund, not Titus.

"This way!" Rosamund's Miniver eyes could obviously see better than Livia's. She grabbed Livia's wrist and they ran through the darkness to the staircase. Livia tripped a second time on the bottom step, but then her hand was on the rail and she was scrambling up the uneven treads with Rosamund in front of her. There were nine steps to the landing, and another nine to the seventh level. Here the darkness was a little less impenetrable, though it was still almost impossible to see. Rosamund tried to run up the next flight of stairs, but Livia suddenly thought of something and pulled her back.

"Not there! Not there, he'll find us!" She dragged Rose

away from the stairs and into the nearest corridor. A lift was there, a document elevator, which carried the files the archivists needed up to the higher levels. It was not meant to carry people, but it would be faster and less obvious than using the stairs. Livia ran her hands along the wall, scraping her fingers on the rough cement. Rosamund almost danced with panic.

"What are you doing? Livia, we need to get out of here!"

"Just hold on!" Livia's hands hit the lift button and a grinding noise sounded in the shaft. The tiny elevator was coming down, level by level. Livia looked anxiously over her shoulder, terrified lest the noise had given them away. At last there was a clunk as the lift arrived. The doors opened slowly, and Livia shoved Rosamund into the gap. The space left was just big enough for her to squeeze into. But when Livia stooped to enter, her body locked up. She began to sweat uncontrollably, and when Rosamund grabbed her arm and tried to pull her in, she fought back, almost without thinking.

"I can't!" she gasped. "I *can't*."

"What do you mean, you can't? It was your idea!" But all Livia's old horror of being shut up had come back, and with it was a new memory; an image of Gibraltar falling, falling, which filled her head with its own particular blackness. Gibraltar had gone to the place from where there was no coming back; and all her pain, and all her struggles had been for nothing. Livia tussled with Rosamund a moment longer, then collapsed to her knees and began to cry.

"It's all over," she said. "It's all over."

Rosamund pulled her quickly into the tiny space. The doors shut behind them, closing Titus out. With a grinding jerk, the lift began to climb.

13

THE MOST SECRET ROOM

The elevator carrying Rosamund and Livia climbed slowly, basement by basement, up through the levels. The motor made an unpleasant grinding noise that reverberated in the enclosed space, and Rosamund could feel it straining under their combined weight. The little lift had been designed for carrying papers, not people, and it was horribly overloaded. Rosamund could hear Livia's laboured breathing: in, out; in, out. Her hand was gripped around Rosamund's arm, and the fingers that dug into her flesh were cold as ice.

It was impossible to say how fast they were travelling. At last the lift bumped to a halt and Rosamund waited for the hiss and scrape of opening doors. Nothing happened, and it was several seconds before it dawned on her that something was wrong. The doors had opened automatically down on the seventh level, but that was not happening here. And, unlike a lift meant for humans, there were no buttons on the inside of the document elevator to open the doors.

Rosamund banged disbelievingly on the door with her fist. Livia was sitting in the corner, her breath coming in great rasping pants. Sweat poured from her, and she was shaking violently. She gasped, "What's the matter?"

"The doors." Rosamund punched them again, and then, bracing her back against the wall, kicked the metal violently with her feet. There was a deafening bang in the enclosed space, and an answering echo from within the shaft. The lift car wobbled unpleasantly. "They're stuck."

"Do you mean we can't get out?" Livia's voice shot up an octave in panic. "Let me out! Let me out! I can't breathe! Let me out, or I'll suffocate." Her arms flailed and she grabbed hold of Rosamund and started banging her against the metal wall. Rosamund struggled helplessly.

"Stop it! Stop it, you're hurting me!"

"I want to get out! I want to get out!"

Rosamund hit her. She did not mean to be cruel, but already she had visions of being trapped inside the little metal box with Livia, until the air ran out. But though a slap on the face always seemed to cure hysterics in movies, it seemed to make no difference now. Livia gave a cry of pain, but did not stop thrashing about.

"We're going to die. We're going to die in here, just

like Gibraltar!"

Rosamund could find no reply. Crazy though Livia was, what she said was right. Unless someone found them quickly, she and Livia would quickly suffocate. Gibraltar's fate had been so terrible that Rosamund had barely started to process it. That something like this might happen to them was more than she could ever have dreamed.

As soon as they left the office containing the Most Secret Room, Emily, Ron and Millamant headed for the main staircase. The sound of clattering boots told them that the guards on the roof were leaving the building, and they waited, just out of sight around the corner, while the troop descended the stairs to the reading room. The last person to pass their hiding place was Trudy. Just as Ron had ordered, she had told her fellow members of Operation Miniver to wait outside the building for further orders.

"I think that should be the last of them," whispered Ron, as Trudy passed from sight. "Come on. We have to get back to the helicopter quickly, before Titus comes back and they realize they've been tricked."

He checked quickly up the stairs and beckoned for

Emily and Millamant to come with him. But as Emily obediently moved to follow, she felt a curious reluctance to leave the building. It was one of those Miniver moments that she could not explain, but that sometimes struck both her and Rosamund when the other was nearby and in danger. It was rather like being on a fishing line that was slowly pulling her in the opposite direction to the one she intended to go.

"Rose," Emily whispered. "She's here."

Ron stopped and looked at her. "What do you mean?" he asked, but Emily had already turned, and was heading not up to the roof, but downstairs in the wake of the retreating guards. That she was putting their escape at risk did not seem to matter to her, and when Ron saw that Millamant was following, running as fast as her stumpy legs could carry her, his protests died. With a last glance up the stairs, he abandoned his attempts to leave, and accompanied the others down the stairs into the reading room.

Emily appeared to know where she was going. She picked her way through the forest of study carrels and emerged at the front reception area. Behind the main desk, a swing door opened on to the archivists' workroom. As Emily leaned her shoulder into the door and pushed it open, Ron thought he heard the sound of muffled banging. He hissed a warning for her to wait, but Emily was already through the door, with Millamant hot on her heels.

Inside was a clutter of desks and trolleys, stacked with files that had come from the basements. The banging sound was louder, and Ron followed his ears to the source. It seemed to be coming from a small lift, at the far end of the room, and the muffled kicks and bangs were interspersed with what sounded like cries for help.

"It's Rose. She's trapped in there!" Emily pressed her fingers repeatedly against the elevator call button, but though the motor hummed, the metal doors remained firmly shut. The lift car had stopped in the shaft, below the level of the floor. Rosamund, if it was really her, was clearly trapped inside.

"Get out of the way." Ron pushed Emily aside, and banged his fist against the metal. The echo reverberated down the shaft, and was met in reply by a perfect frenzy of shrieks and bangs. A girl's voice called faintly, "Let us out! Let us out!" Emily tensed. The voice was unmistakably Rosamund's.

"Don't worry, Rose! We're going to save you!"

There was a tinkle of glass behind her. Millamant had smashed the cover on the fire hydrant, and came hurrying back with a small axe. Ron seized it and started smashing at the lift. The first few blows bounced off noisily, but then he managed to force the blade of the axe between the metal doors and started levering them open. Emily could hear the screams from the lift car getting louder.

"It's us, Rose! Don't worry, we're nearly there."

Something in the door mechanism gave way with a loud snap. The doors went loose in their track and Ron grabbed hold of them with both hands and pushed them apart. The floor of the lift car had stopped a little way below the floor level, leaving a narrow gap between the workroom floor and the car's roof. Ron lay down and thrust his arm inside. He grunted, and began to pull. Emily and Millamant watched breathlessly as a small hand appeared, gripped tight around Ron's forearm, and then the top of a tousled head. Rosamund's face followed, grimacing as she squeezed through the gap. A moment later, she rolled out and collapsed on the floor in front of them, covered in dust and filth. When she saw Emily, her face was transformed with joy, and she burst into tears.

"Emmie, you're alive! Primrose told me you were dead, but I couldn't believe it!"

Emily made a choking sound. She shook her head and reached out her arms, and then Rosamund saw Millamant and cried out again. Meanwhile, Ron was doing his best to haul Livia out of the lift car. It was much harder to get her out, because she was a normal size, and the space she had to squeeze through was a small one. Her face was red and streaked with tears and when Ron finally succeeded in dragging her free, she began to fight him, punching and kicking him until he let her go.

"Don't touch me! Get away from me!"

"Livia!" exclaimed Emily. "What's the matter?"

"*You're* the matter." Livia backed away, her voice so thick with emotion they could barely understand what she was saying. "The Minivers are the matter. Ask *her*." She pointed to Rosamund. "Ask her how she killed Gibraltar. But don't ask me to do anything for you ever again!"

"Livia, please—" Emily reached out a hand, but Livia was blundering away from her. She disappeared between the trolleys, and the swing door on to the reading room flapped open and closed.

"That's it," said Ron. "Come on. We have to get up to the roof now, as quickly as we can."

Livia ran. She did not know where she was heading, but she knew she had to get away from the Minivers. Her head was jumbled with frightful thoughts of the ninth basement and Rosamund's stupidity; of Titus, looking like a fallen angel, and Gibraltar as he plunged into darkness. The sound of the guards assembling in the Archives foyer drove her away from the front entrance, and sent her running up the stairs instead. She rounded a corner and cannoned into someone coming in the opposite direction. Livia scarcely even noticed who it was until she spoke.

"Livia!" Madame drew back a little. Livia looked so alarming that for a moment she did not know whether or not she intended to attack her. "What are you doing here? What's the matter?"

Livia shook her head. She could not speak, and Madame, who was not a particularly sympathetic person, was staggered when her cousin flung herself into her arms. Livia herself could not have said why she did this. Perhaps it was Madame's strange, fleeting family resemblance to her own dead mother; or perhaps she was simply so bereft and despairing that she would have reached out to anyone. But if Livia was amazed at her reaction, Madame amazed herself even more. No one had embraced her since she was a little girl. When Livia reached out, Madame put her bony arms around her cousin's body, and held her in an unnatural gesture of comfort.

"My dear." The word "dear" was one Madame had rarely uttered, except when complaining of the ruinous expense of things. "My dear, whatever is the matter? Is it –" Madame had a sudden brainwave. "Is it Titus?"

Livia gave a sob. Taking this to mean yes, Madame went on, "Titus is an evil creature. We must do our best to stop him, mustn't we?"

Livia nodded. It was what Gibraltar had said, that Titus must be stopped. Her eyes flooded with tears again, and she was struggling to control them when she became aware that Madame was staring at the neck of her T-shirt. Livia looked down. In the course of her underground adventures, the chain on which she had hung the half-key to the Most Secret Room had worked its way out from under her collar and was clearly visible against the pale material.

"What's that key, Livia dear?"

"It's Grandfather's," Livia whispered. "I found it in the garage at Daventry Street."

Madame stared at the key. It was, without doubt, the original of the wax copy her mother had used to get into the Most Secret Room, and that she had destroyed to stop Titus from finding it. "Will you – give it to me?"

Livia closed her hand defensively around the key. She had not intended to tell Madame she had it. A memory stirred, of the house in Daventry Street and what

Madame had done to it. Then she pushed it down. After what she had witnessed in the basements, what had happened to a house hardly seemed to matter. What mattered to her now was revenge.

"Show me the Most Secret Room, first," she said. 'I want to see where it is."

"Of course." Madame had no wish to share her discovery, but since the location of the Most Secret Room was no longer a secret, the most important thing was to get into it before anybody else. Madame put on a smile that was meant to be friendly, but made her look like a piranha. "Come with me."

She led Livia along the passage to the senior staff offices. It was one of the few parts of the building Livia had been unable to search, and explained why her attempts to find the Most Secret Room in the basements had failed. A little bit of Livia felt angry that she had wasted so much time down there, but she did not let on to Madame. All she wanted now was to punish Rosamund Miniver, and to do that, she had to get into the Most Secret Room.

Madame led Livia into the office where she had rolled back the carpet. She pointed out the keyhole in the floor. "There it is."

Livia knelt and unhooked the key from around her neck. Her fingers brushed the tiny keyhole, and she wondered how she would ever have found it, even if she had known where to look. Livia inserted the half-key into the lock, but it wobbled and would not turn by itself. She pulled it out again. She and Madame were standing together, staring at the keyhole in frustration, when a voice spoke unexpectedly behind them.

"How kind of you to find it for me," said Titus.

Livia whirled, the adrenaline jolt almost knocking her off her feet. She saw Titus moving towards them, and then everything happened so quickly that her cry of shock was cut off. With a strength that must have come from sheer desperation, Madame snatched up an office chair and swung it at Titus's head. The metal legs caught his skull with an audible crack, and he fell like a stone to the floor.

"Is he – dead?" asked Livia, in a wavering voice. Emily and Rosamund's stories about Titus had frightened her for so long now that she had almost come to believe he had supernatural powers. She could not believe that he had tracked her all the way from the basements. Madame, who had been expecting him to come back to the Archivist's office sooner or later, walked over and gave him a kick in the ribs. Unlike Trudy, she had swung her weapon with the intention of doing maximum damage. Titus was certainly not dead, but it was clear that she had knocked him out cold.

"He'll live," said Madame. "What matters now is the Most Secret Room." She dropped to her knees and pulled at Titus's collar. A half-key was hanging around his neck on a metal chain, almost identical to the one Livia was holding. Madame snapped the chain and held out her hand to Livia.

"Give me yours."

Livia shook her head. Some sort of sense was belatedly returning to her, but Madame was fed up with last-minute interference. She lunged at Livia. There was a brief, futile struggle, a cry of pain, and Livia dropped her key on the floor. Madame snatched it up. The two halves of the key clicked together. Madame inserted them into the lock and, with a soft *thunk*, the key turned and the mechanism released the secret trapdoor. Madame grabbed hold of its edge and swung back the flap.

"Come on," she said impatiently. "After the time you've spent looking for this, I'd have thought you'd be more interested."

Livia moved to the edge of the hole. She felt the cold of stonework below her, and smelled glue and paper. A metal staircase, steep as a ladder, led downwards, and she glimpsed red boxes, piled on shelves along the walls of a long narrow room. Livia began to shake. She did not want to go down into the darkness. Yet, somewhere inside those boxes was the information they all wanted: the answers to all their questions about Artemisia's past and future, and to many other questions they had not even thought to ask.

Madame was already disappearing into the hole. With a backwards glance at Titus's motionless body, Livia put her foot on the ladder and began to descend.

The rooftop appeared deserted. *Emily-Rose* sat where they had left it. Ron made the girls and Millamant wait on the staircase while he went to check the helicopter over, but it seemed Trudy had followed his orders to the letter. Ron beckoned to the others, and they hurried across the roof and climbed inside.

Millamant got into the seat beside Ron, and Emily and Rosamund took their places in the passenger cabin, ready for take-off. While Ron ran through the cockpit checks, Emily turned to Rosamund.

"Is it true?" she said. "Is Gibraltar really dead?"

It was the question Rosamund had been dreading. In the aftermath of Gibraltar's plunge, every instinct had been concerned with her own survival, and she had done little more than react. But now the shock had caught up with her, and she could not dodge reality any longer. Emily had feelings too, and her question must be answered.

"I don't know," said Rosamund. "You see – we were down in the eighth basement. It was so dark and dreadful there. Gibraltar was trying to talk Titus into giving up. He was trying to tell him something important; something he knew about Titus's parents; but Titus wouldn't listen. They were fighting, right on the edge, and then I saw— I saw—" Rosamund broke off. It was as if the essence, the very soul of her, had fallen into the ninth basement with Gibraltar, and was wandering, lost in the darkness. It would be doing that, she knew, for a very long time. "Gibraltar fell, Emmie. He just – fell."

Emily wanted to cry. Later, she knew she probably would, but the look on Rosamund's face was so bleak, so despairing, that she dared not let herself. If ever there was a time to give up and run away, it was now. But Emily knew instinctively that they must not. If they did, if she let Rosamund give into the impulse, they would be finished.

"We have *Emily-Rose*," said Emily. "We're together. We may have lost Livia and Gibraltar but we have Millamant again, and Ron. The fight isn't over, Rose. We have to make what happened to Gibraltar count. And we can't do that until there's a Miniver on the throne of Artemisia."

Rosamund nodded. The grief was not gone, of course. In the days to come, she would take it up again many times, and each time she would find her loss a little more final, a little more real. Eventually, one day in the distant future, she might even understand, but for now, Emily was right. There was only one thing she could do.

Ron leaned over from the cockpit. "Where to, ladies?"

Rosamund slipped off her seatbelt and stood up. "It's time to mobilize the fans," she said. "We've been hiding for long enough. Collect Lindsey and Fiona, and take us to the Artemisia Hotel."

The helicopter rose from the Archives rooftop and flew away. It circled the city, the river and the hospital where Ron's son Alex was recovering from his operation. It flew over the Parliament and what was left of Miniver House. In his hospital room at the Artemisia Palace, Papa King lay quietly under the bedsheets. His eyes were closed and his breathing was shallow. What thoughts were passing through his head nobody could have told. They might have been of the past or the future; of Madame, the Minivers, or even Gibraltar. As the helicopter passed overhead, his eyes opened briefly, and what might have been a smile passed over his face.

Then, as the sound of the rotors faded into the distance, they closed again, and his breathing slowed and stopped.

The battle for the throne of Artemisia had begun.

the MINIVERS
MINI princesses, BIG adventures

Meet the Minivers · About the author · The story so far · Books · Fun · Competition

Meet the Minivers – Artemisia's brightest stars!

Hi, I'm Rosamund!

Thank you so much for visiting our website. Shall I tell you a bit about myself?

I'm 14 - I think - I was discovered in a shoebox outside the Artemisia Hospital as a baby, and Papa King has looked after me ever since. He named me after his mother, Queen Rosamund, and he chose my surname, Miniver, because I'm so tiny - I'm a mini version of a person. My sister Emily and I are both only two feet tall! We are really busy these days, designing clothes for our own fashion label, working on our TV show, and our music has really taken off. We are having a fantastic time, and really appreciate the support of you, our fans.

Hello, I'm Emily!

I was found on the steps of Miniver House as a baby - although I often wonder where I came from. I'm so happy to live here with Papa King and Rosamund... I couldn't ask for a more loving family. Rosamund and I have sung together for as long as I can remember... have you heard our new album, Minivers Together or our number 1 single Sisters Forever is taken from there. I would love to hear what you think. We have some new perfumes out too - look out for them. We both hope you enjoy looking round our site. Come back often as you can!

THE STORY SO [FAR]

ABANDONED!

Mystery surrounds the origins of a miniature baby girl discovered in a shoebox outside the Artemisia Hospital on Thursday night. The newborn, who weighs about as much as a block of butter, is in excellent health and was rushed to doctors, who ran four tests for her overnight.

The baby, who under the hearts of Artemisians, with doctor of Artemisia already offering to take her. Miniverhood, the hospital matron already offering to take her. Few parents to come forward.

MINIATURE BABY HEADED FOR PALACE!

It's official: in a move that will disappoint hundreds of hopeful families, Papa King announced last night that he will be fostering Artemisia's famous miniature orphan himself.

'It's my job to look after all disadvantaged citizens,' the King said. 'I am determined that this tiny abandoned baby will have the chance she deserves. Artemisia's tiniest new baby has already been given a new baby's name. From now on the little orphan will be called Rosamund, after his mother, and Miniver because she is a miniature version of a human being.

A sister for Rosamund

Now there are two of us! Artemisia's darling, Rosamund Miniver, has a new sister, Emily, who was found in a basket on the steps of Miniver House yesterday morning.

The baby is absolutely gorgeous, and excited foster father Papa King, Rosamund is so excited, she wept. I adore the name Emily alone. Now there's another Miniver for Artemisians to love.

It's a Miniver Morning

'Miniver Morning', Rosamund Miniver's first single, has debuted at Number 1 in the Artemisia charts.

'I'd like to dedicate the song to my little sister, Emily,' Rosamund told Pop Music Weekly. The miniature pop star ruled out the possibility of a concert tour, as four-year-old Emily is too young to go with her. 'We Minivers do everything together,' Rosamund said. 'I won't travel anywhere without Emily. It would be awful!'

Emily
Sweet and fresh as a Miniver Morning
A new perfume from Delaney's of Queen Street

MINIVER HOUSE [ ] SETS NEW TRE[ND]

PINK IS THE NEW C[OLOUR] home this morning with the glossy announcement that of Miniver House is being repainted in blush pink. The miniature sisters also [ ] where new non-coloured [ ] will be highlighted by white. Rumour has it that who favour bold colours, in yellow and gold furnishings, gorgeous tastes bedrooms. Minivers do everything together. Emily's room is being match in her favourite car.

HIT MINIVER TV SERIES RETUR[NS]

CHANNEL 4 has confirmed that the smash-hit series of Artemisia's another set of episodes of The Miniver store in the new year. That third series successful programmes will show the performing on stage and give news on glamorous of the fantastic twins private life. Filming has already begun first episode will be shown in early Febru[ary]

the MINIVERS

Visit our cool website
to find out what we've
been up to lately!

www.theminivers.co.uk

Out now!

Natalie Jane Prior

the

MiNiVERS

ON THE RUN

MINI princesses, BIG adventures

And coming soon. . .

Natalie Jane Prior

The MINIVERS RULE!

MINI princesses, BIG adventures